I0600490

Pajama Tops

A Play in Three Acts

by Mawby Green and Ed Feilbert

Based on the French Farce
Moumou
by Jean de Letraz

A SAMUEL FRENCH ACTING EDITION

SAMUEL FRENCH

FOUNDED 1830

New York Hollywood London Toronto

SAMUELFRENCH.COM

Copyright © 1945 by Jean de Letraz as an unpublished play under the title
MOUMOU
Copyright © 1954 by Eric Mawby Green and Jean de Letraz as an unpublished play,
under the title PAJAMA TOPS
Copyright © 1982 Eric Mawby Green
Copyright © 1948 by Eric Mawby Green and Jean de Letraz as an unpublished play,
under the title MISTER IN-BETWEEN
Copyright © 1975 In Renewal by Eric Mawby Green and Simone de Letraz as an
unpublished play, under the title MISTER IN-BETWEEN

ALL RIGHTS RESERVED

CAUTION: Professionals and amateurs are hereby warned that *PAJAMA TOPS* is sub-
ject to a Licensing Fee. It is fully protected under the copyright laws of the United
States of America, the British Commonwealth, including Canada, and all other coun-
tries of the Copyright Union. All rights, including professional, amateur, motion
picture, recitation, lecturing, public reading, radio broadcasting, television and the
rights of translation into foreign languages are strictly reserved. In its present form
the play is dedicated to the reading public only.

The amateur live stage performance rights to *PAJAMA TOPS* are controlled exclusively by Samuel French, Inc., and licensing arrangements and performance licenses
must be secured well in advance of presentation. PLEASE NOTE that amateur Licensing Fees are set upon application in accordance with your producing circumstances.
When applying for a licensing quotation and a performance license please give us the
number of performances intended, dates of production, your seating capacity and
admission fee. Licensing Fees are payable one week before the opening performance
of the play to Samuel French, Inc., at 45 W. 25th Street, New York, NY 10010.

Licensing Fee of the required amount must be paid whether the play is presented
for charity or gain and whether or not admission is charged.

Stock licensing fees quoted upon application to Samuel French, Inc.

For all other rights than those stipulated above, apply to: Samuel French, Inc.

Particular emphasis is laid on the question of amateur or professional readings,
permission and terms for which must be secured in writing from Samuel French, Inc.

Copying from this book in whole or in part is strictly forbidden by law, and the
right of performance is not transferable.

Whenever the play is produced the following notice must appear on all programs,
printing and advertising for the play: "Produced by special arrangement with Samuel
French, Inc."

Due authorship credit must be given on all programs, printing and advertising for
the play.

No one shall commit or authorize any act or omission by which the
copyright of, or the right to copyright, this play may be impaired.

No one shall make any changes in this play for the purpose of
production.

Publication of this play does not imply availability for performance. Both
amateurs and professionals considering a production are strongly advised in
their own interests to apply to Samuel French, Inc., for written permission
before starting rehearsals, advertising, or booking a theatre.

No part of this book may be reproduced, stored in a retrieval system, or
transmitted in any form, by any means, now known or yet to be invented,
including mechanical, electronic, photocopying, recording, videotaping, or
otherwise, without the prior written permission of the publisher.

ISBN   978-0-573-61439-2   Printed   in   U.S.A.   #837

THE CHARACTERS IN THE PLAY

CLAUDINE

INSPECTOR LEGRAND

YVONNE CHAUVINET

GEORGES CHAUVINET

LEONARD JOLIJOLI

BABETTE LATOUCHE

JACQUES

* * *

The entire action takes place in the living room of the villa "Clair de Lune" in Deauville, France. The time is the present.

ACT ONE

An afternoon in August.

ACT TWO

One hour later.

ACT THREE

The next morning.

Pajama Tops

ACT ONE

The living room of the villa "Clair de Lune" in Deau-
ville. Upstage Left there is an arch to hall with a
few steps going up to the bedrooms. This hall also
leads to the front door of the villa. Door Down-
stage Left leads to study; door Downstage Right
to dining room and kitchen. French windows
Upstage Right lead to garden and beach. Against
wall, between arch and door Downstage Left, is
a bar and bar stool. The sofa is Right Center and
an armchair is few feet Left. A straightback
chair is next to door Downstage Left, its mate
next to door Downstage Right. The furnishings
are bright and summery.

An afternoon in August. The curtain rises; the door-
bell tinkles. There is a pause of three beats, then
CLAUDINE *comes bouncing out door Downstage*
Right and bounces across the room to answer the
door. CLAUDINE *has a lot to bounce with.*

INSPECTOR. (*Offstage.*) I'm Inspector Legrand . . .
of the Deauville Police.
   CLAUDINE. (*Offstage.*) Come in, Inspector! (CLAU-
DINE *re-enters, followed by* INSPECTOR LEGRAND, *wear-*
ing khaki shorts, khaki jacket and a pith helmet. He
might be on a safari. Getting a good look at CLAU-
DINE'S *scanty attire, the* INSPECTOR *pauses. He is in*
his sixties, with a twinkle in his eyes and those eyes
for women.) Please do. Now, what can I do for you?
   INSPECTOR. Well, er . . .
   CLAUDINE. Yes, Inspector?

INSPECTOR. Well, er . . . is anybody home?

CLAUDINE. Only the Madame.

INSPECTOR. I'd like to see her.

CLAUDINE. She's undressing .

INSPECTOR. I'd still like to see her.

CLAUDINE. She's putting on her bikini.

INSPECTOR. Well, that's better than nothing! (*With a chuckle.*) What am I saying!

CLAUDINE. Would you care for a drink?

INSPECTOR. No, thank you.

CLAUDINE. A cigarette?

INSPECTOR. No, thank you. I have this. (*Takes out cigar.*)

CLAUDINE. Ooh! (*Picks up lighter.*) Let me light it for you, Inspector. (*Lights his cigar.*) There! (*Remains close to him.*)

INSPECTOR. You're really most obliging.

CLAUDINE. (*Replacing lighter.*) Oh, that's nothing. Really nothing.

INSPECTOR. I wouldn't say that. (*Sits sofa.*) What's your name?

CLAUDINE. Claudine . . . Claudine Amour.

INSPECTOR. Claudine Amour. It fits you to a tee.

CLAUDINE. You think so? (*Jumps on sofa, on her knees facing him.*)

INSPECTOR. Oh, yes! . . . Have you been here long?

CLAUDINE. In this house? (*As though it were ten years.*) A whole month! (*Squirming on sofa, physically restless.*) Isn't that dreadful!

INSPECTOR. I see you don't like to stay in the same position too long.

CLAUDINE. I'm here merely to finish up my studies. I'm preparing myself for a very delicate profession.

INSPECTOR. Yes? And what profession . . . (CLAUDINE *pokes him with her shoes.*) Oooh! Watch those heels! And what profession would that be?

CLAUDINE. Oh, how can you describe it? Words are so inadequate. You can't say cocotte . . .

INSPECTOR. Why not? Cocotte . . . prostitute . . . hooker . . .

CLAUDINE. Really, Inspector! The words you choose. This is *not* the oldest profession. It's quite superior. I want to become a grande courtesan . . . like Madame DuBarry!

INSPECTOR. Call the song what you like but the tune is still played on the same instrument.

CLAUDINE. Oh, I'm disappointed in you, Inspector. You have no sense of nuance. Look at me. I've studied astrology . . . numerology . . . even demonology.

INSPECTOR. No!

CLAUDINE. Yes! I can raise the devil!

INSPECTOR. You don't say! (*Puts his hand on her knee.*)

CLAUDINE. I once kept house for an antique dealer and what I don't know about old pieces isn't worth knowing. (*She removes his hand and he slaps his knee in disappointment. She rises.*) I have been a model, studied art, music, literature . . .

INSPECTOR. All that, and what are you now?

CLAUDINE. At the moment, personal maid to Madame Chauvinet . . . one of the most fashionable women in Deauville. She's taught me how to give an intimate supper for two or a banquet for a hundred. I'm equipped to receive the very best people . . . shahs and sheiks, ambassadors and bishops.

INSPECTOR. Do you expect to receive many bishops?

CLAUDINE. In my profession, a girl must be prepared to entertain anyone. All I'm waiting for now is the opportunity.

INSPECTOR. Ah, if I were twenty years younger . . .

CLAUDINE. You would still be wasting your time, Inspector. A policeman can guard a special jewel but he certainly can't afford one.

INSPECTOR. My dear, I can't even . . . I'm like this cigar here.

CLAUDINE. How's that, Inspector?

INSPECTOR. Burned out.

CLAUDINE. All you need is a little light, m'sieur (*Gets lighter from table and crosses to* INSPECTOR.)

INSPECTOR. Light, hell! Even a bonfire wouldn't help me!

CLAUDINE. (*Laughs and returns the lighter.*) What I need is to make a splash . . . get myself talked about . . . my picture in the papers! That's the only way to start a career . . . cause a sensation!

INSPECTOR. Ah, what you need is publicity.

CLAUDINE. Yes, what I need is a nice notorious scandal!

INSPECTOR. It seems we have something in common.

CLAUDINE. (*Behind the sofa, over his shoulder.*) We do?

INSPECTOR. (*Confidentially.*) I'm in exactly the same position as you!

CLAUDINE. What? You want to become a grande courtesan too?

INSPECTOR. Yes! . . . No! No, no, no, no, no. I'm not the type. But in order to finish my career in a blaze of glory, I need a notorious scandal to break my way too. And there's a chance . . . a small chance . . .

CLAUDINE. (*Eagerly.*) Yes, Inspector? (*Comes round the sofa and sits next to the* INSPECTOR.)

INSPECTOR. (*Taking out envelope from pocket.*) I have just received this report. A much wanted swindler is heading in this direction. He may be in Deauville now. He may be . . .

CLAUDINE. (*Putting her forehead next to his.*) Oh, we must put our heads together, my sweet, sweet Inspector. Who knows? We may be able to help each other!

INSPECTOR. Well, I'll certainly do my part. (YVONNE CHAUVINET *in a bikini enters from hall. He rises.*) Ah! Madame Chauvinet . . .

YVONNE. Inspector Legrand. How nice!

INSPECTOR. The pleasure's mine, madame. (*Kisses her hand.*)

YVONNE. (*Spotting* CLAUDINE *on sofa.*) Claudine!
(*To* INSPECTOR.) Excuse me just a moment. (*Crosses
to* CLAUDINE.) Comfortable?

CLAUDINE. Very.

YVONNE. That's a pretty nothing you're wearing.

CLAUDINE. Oh, thank you!

YVONNE. But it's not your uniform!

CLAUDINE. (*Rises.*) Oh! Yes, madame . . . I mean
no, madame . . . I'll take it off right now! (*Starts to
remove her "nothing."*)

YVONNE. And bring me my beach bag . . . immediately!

CLAUDINE. Yes, madame! (*Exits hall.*)

YVONNE. I must apologize for my maid. I can't
imagine what you must think of her.

INSPECTOR. Don't try, madame. But I don't think she
did me any harm.

YVONNE. You wish to speak to me, Inspector?

INSPECTOR. I really came to see Monsieur Chauvinet
. . . but it can wait. You certainly look ravishing in
that bikini.

YVONNE. (*Amused . . . an old game with an old
friend.*) Flatterer!

INSPECTOR. And if I were twenty years younger . . .

YVONNE. I should still be playing with my doll . . .

INSPECTOR. That's true.

YVONNE. Can I offer you anything else?

INSPECTOR. No, madame. So far they haven't discovered a substitute. I'll drop back later to see your
husband, if I won't be disturbing you.

YVONNE. (*Extending her hand.*) Anytime. You're
always welcome, Inspector.

INSPECTOR. (*Kissing her hand but keeping his eyes
on the bikini.*) And I hope to see more of you
later . . .

YVONNE. Yes . . . (*Reacts, then laughs.*) Really,
Inspector!

INSPECTOR. (*Waving.*) So long . . . for now! (*He
eyes* CLAUDINE *entering, then exits hall.*)

CLAUDINE. Your bag, madame.

YVONNE. So, you entertain my visitors . . .

CLAUDINE. No, madame. I was only practising!

YVONNE. The way you practise on my husband, I suppose. (GEORGES CHAUVINET *enters from the study, carrying a small valise. He is about forty, a man who likes to have things comfortable and abhors complications. In excellent spirits, he is humming as he enters.*) Oh, there you are, dear!

GEORGES. Yes, angel.

YVONNE. You just missed Inspector Legrand.

GEORGES. Oh? Anything up?

YVONNE. Not really. He just looked in. He'll be back.

GEORGES. Good. (*Crosses to* CLAUDINE.) Claudine?

CLAUDINE. Yes, m'sieur?

GEORGES. Will you pack my bag as usual?

CLAUDINE. Yes, m'sieur.

GEORGES. Then put it in my car.

CLAUDINE. Yes, m'sieur.

GEORGES. And please hurry!

CLAUDINE. Yes, m'sieur. (*Starts to leave, then stops.*) Oh, I'm sorry, m'sieur, but I can't.

GEORGES. Can't?

CLAUDINE. It's time for a lesson. Today my guru is going to get me in the lotus position.

GEORGES. Claudine, you have a week's notice!

CLAUDINE. Oh! (*Exits hall.*)

YVONNE. You'd better call the agency again about that butler.

GEORGES. All right. I will. Later.

YVONNE. Aren't you coming swimming with me?

GEORGES. I'd love to, Yvonne . . . but how can I? I have to make this trip.

YVONNE. My poor darling! Must you work so hard, even in August?

GEORGES. Can't neglect our business! And I believe

Latouche is finally . . . you know who I mean . . . my good friend Latouche . . . ?

YVONNE. Yes, yes, I know. Latouche from Bayeux.

GEORGES. That's right. I believe he's going to help me expand the business. Wants to handle our products throughout Normandie. And with his new branches . . .

YVONNE. (*Pouting.*) Oh, bother his new branches . . .

GEORGES. Now, now, Yvonne.

YVONNE. What time shall I expect you back then tonight?

GEORGES. (*Trying to be off-handed.*) Oh . . . certainly after dinner . . . unless Latouche wants me to spend the night.

YVONNE. You don't sound very sorry about having to leave me for a whole night.

GEORGES. How can you say that? (*Placing his finger first on her nose then on her breasts.*) To have to leave this . . . and this . . . and this. Darling, isn't this bikini a trifle . . . a trifle too . . .

YVONNE. A trifle too . . . what?

GEORGES. Revealing.

YVONNE. Jealous?

GEORGES. Well, it's always dangerous to excite the appetite of hungry eyes.

YVONNE. If I make you peckish, darling, why don't you take a nibble before you go?

GEORGES. Oh, Yvonne, if only there were time! Good God! Do you realize what time it is?

YVONNE. (*Picks up beach bag and towel.*) All right, Georges. You win for now. But don't go rushing off until I've had my swim! I have a wonderful surprise for you!

GEORGES. Surprise? What is it, my sweet?

YVONNE. Promise you won't leave until I get back?

GEORGES. All right, I promise. Well, what's the surprise?

YVONNE. You'll see, darling! You'll see! (*Exits French windows laughing.*)

GEORGES. Damn! I'll never get away! (*Looks at watch and crosses to bar to phone.*)

CLAUDINE. (*She enters from hall.*) Ssst! Are you alone?

GEORGES. Not anymore.

CLAUDINE. (*Digging into bodice of her low cut uniform.*) I have something for you . . .

GEORGES. (*Alarmed.*) Claudine!

CLAUDINE. (*Taking out letter.*) This letter. It's marked "Strictly Personal."

GEORGES. (*Takes letter; looks at envelope.*) Why it's from an old friend.

CLAUDINE. (*Wisely.*) Of course, m'sieur. Who else?

GEORGES. From an *old friend!* Besides it's none of your business!

CLAUDINE. (*Going to him provocatively as she practises her "profession."*) Must you make this trip, m'sieur?

GEORGES. What do you mean?

CLAUDINE. Well . . . sometimes you can do quite as much . . . business . . . at home, if you know where to look.

GEORGES. Perhaps it's just that I enjoy doing business with certain people.

CLAUDINE. (*Thwarted.*) Business business? Is that what you're talking about?

GEORGES. Aren't you, Claudine?

CLAUDINE. Now you're laughing at me. You think you're very superior! But let me tell you . . .

GEORGES. You're a babe in the woods . . . a diamond in the rough . . .

CLAUDINE. (*Crossing to hall.*) Oh, am I? Well, the day will come when you'll regret not having polished . . . this diamond in the rough! (*Flounces out.* GEORGES *laughs, then sees the letter in his hand and it sobers him.*)

GEORGES. (*Opens letter.*) Well, I'll be damned! It's from Leonard . . . Leonard Jolijoli!

(LEONARD *flies in through the French windows. Peter Pan couldn't do better.* LEONARD *is charming, the aesthetic type.*)

LEONARD. That's right . . . and here I am!

GEORGES. Where did you come from?

LEONARD. The garden.

GEORGES. What were you doing out there?

LEONARD. Oh, Georges, I was hiding! In your rhododendrons! I didn't want to meet a living soul. I only wanted to speak to you. The most horrible thing has happened to me. I'm all aflutter! (*Snatches drink from* GEORGES *and takes quick gulp.*) Thank you.

GEORGES. First, tell me, where have you been all these years?

LEONARD. Traveling! Pago-Pago, Bora-Bora, Fiji-Wiji!

GEORGES. Fiji-Wiji. What were you doing in Fiji?

LEONARD. Chasing poetry!

GEORGES. Poetry! And you're back now on a visit?

LEONARD. No. I'm through with the Pearls of the Pacific . . . for good. I was disillusioned . . .

GEORGES. By a little native girl?

LEONARD. . . . disillusioned frightfully . . .

GEORGES. You didn't marry her, did you?

LEONARD. Oh, no! . . . My friend did. I'm single. I've discovered that women . . . all women . . . want to devour the male. They're materialistic, grasping, caustic, self-centered . . .

GEORGES. Yes, but so adorable!

LEONARD. They don't understand me.

GEORGES. You were never easy to understand, Leonard.

LEONARD. I know. I know. But there should be one woman interested in my *soul*, too. Friendship, Georges . . . what I feel for you . . . is the only thing you can depend on.

GEORGES. Well, since you hate women so . . . I'd better confess I'm married to one!

LEONARD. No need to apologize. Marriage is good for you. You're different. You're a business man. What's your wife like?

GEORGES. She's a beautiful person!

LEONARD. Oh, one of those.

GEORGES. (*Angrily.*) No, she's not one of those! She's luscious, toothsome, the most delicious, the most delectable . . .

LEONARD. Oh, are we having her for dinner, Georges?

GEORGES. (*Exasperatedly.*) What's this horrible thing that's happened to you?

LEONARD. Oh, yes. But first, I must tell you, I've written a tragedy . . . in verse . . . something in the manner of Shakespeare . . . and I have a letter of introduction to the Director of the Comedie-Francaise!

GEORGES. Well?

LEONARD. Don't you see? Once he discovers I can write like Shakespeare . . . only Shakespeare's dead and I'm alive . . . they'll produce it . . . and I'll be made . . . made! . . . in the only other way I dream of being made!

GEORGES. All right, so you're a success. But let's get back to the rhododendrons.

LEONARD. (*Taking stage.*) Oh yes. Something dreadful's happened to me! Last night after finishing my new poem . . . "Cornucopia" . . .

GEORGES. "Cornucopia?"

LEONARD. The horn of plenty. I was dying to share it with someone and at my very first bar, I met a young man. His name was Zizi. A swimming instructor. He was amazingly well versed in the Arts.

GEORGES. And you shared your "Cornucopia" with him?

LEONARD. Yes! And he was so taken with it, he wanted to share everything else I had! Written. It was only after he'd gone that I discovered he had also taken my wallet. (*Sits chair Right Center.*)

GEORGES. Zizi come . . . Zizi go.

LEONARD. But he took everything . . . my money, my passport, my poems, my Identity Card! I can't even prove who I am!

GEORGES. Have you told the police about it?

LEONARD. Oh, for heaven's sake, no! Who knows what kind of story that Zizi might tell them? Then farewell Comedie-Francaise!

GEORGES. Why?

LEONARD. Don't you see? They'd never touch me if I was tinged with scandal. No, nobody must know what happened. Georges, my life, my future, are in your hands!

GEORGES. What can I do for you?

LEONARD. Lend me a few hundred francs.

GEORGES. Gladly . . .

LEONARD. And let me stay here for a few days!

GEORGES. That I can't do.

LEONARD. No? Why?

GEORGES. Well, since you've confided in me . . .

LEONARD. Yes?

GEORGES. Are you discreet?

LEONARD. As an orchid in the moonlight!

GEORGES. Well . . . er . . . the fact is . . . I have a little bit of business to attend to in Bayeux.

LEONARD. I thought you adored your wife?

GEORGES. I do . . . but not exclusively.

LEONARD. Your poor wife.

GEORGES. Look, Leonard, I'm only doing this so I don't appear ridiculous.

LEONARD. Ridiculous? How's that?

GEORGES. Well, if a husband cheats on his wife first, he doesn't look like a fool if she cheats on him later.

LEONARD. Oh, yes. I see. That's very good. Do I know this bitch? . . . er . . . *bit* of business in Bayeux? I sort of pushed them together.

GEORGES. No. I only met her six weeks ago, (*Rhapsodically.*) Babette Latouche . . . !

LEONARD. Babette Latouche?

GEORGES. Such a beautiful creature! So lush, so desirable! Why, she's got . . . (*Cups his hands in front of his chest as if he were holding huge melons.*)

LEONARD. Arthritis?

GEORGES. And she's promised me that tonight is going to be our night.

LEONARD. Your wife lets you sleep out?

GEORGES. Of course. I tell her I'm going to see my old friend Latouche . . . an invaluable business associate.

LEONARD. (*Surprised.*) Then your Babette is *his* wife?

GEORGES. No. She has no husband. Latouche doesn't exist. He's someone I invented.

LEONARD. Invented? Ooh! What if your wife finds out?

GEORGES. My God! Don't even think of it! I know Yvonne. Before leaving me, she'd have her revenge.

LEONARD. Revenge?

GEORGES. She'd take a lover!

LEONARD. Why should that bother you if you're deceiving her first?

GEORGES. That's just it. I haven't deceived her yet.

LEONARD. But what if this Babette of yours should turn up here?

GEORGES. That would be a calamity! Babette doesn't know I'm married. (*Sigh of relief.*) But she won't show up. How can she? I never told her I had a villa in Deauville!

LEONARD. Then you're not going to ask me to stay? (*Plucks flower from bunch in vase.*)

GEORGES. How can I! I don't even have a butler to leave you with. (*Going to phone.*) That reminds me . . . I've got to call the agency.

LEONARD. (*Stopping him.*) Georges, you can't leave me in this fix! I'll dash over to the hotel, get my bag and . . .

GEORGES. No!

LEONARD. It will only take a minute!

GEORGES. No, Leonard! It's impossible. But I'll tell you what I will do.

LEONARD. What?

GEORGES. I'll call Inspector Legrand. He's a personal friend of mine. I'll tell him about Zizi beating it with your wallet.

LEONARD. You'll tell him no such thing! (*Rushes to French windows.*) I'll be back before you know it, Georges.

GEORGES. No, Leonard! You can't! You're taking advantage of my friendship!

LEONARD. Oh, don't say that, Georges! Remember . . . friendship is sweeter even than love . . . and a damn sight less chancey! (*Gives plucked flower to* GEORGES.) Bye! Bye! (*Exits quickly.*)

GEORGES. (*Running after him.*) Leonard! Listen . . . (*Seeing him disappear.*) Damn! This would have to happen today! (*Going to phone.*) The hell with Zizi, Shakespeare *and* the Comedie-Francaise! (*Into receiver.*) Hello? Hello? Deauville 567. (YVONNE, *laughing and carrying beach towel, enters through French windows. Without covering the receiver.*) Oh! Be careful! You're wetting the floor! . . . No, no, not you, operator! (YVONNE *laughs.*) . . . Is this the Superior Domestic Agency? This is Monsieur Chauvinet, Villa Clair de Lune. Have you found me an experienced butler yet? . . . Well, if one should turn up, you have the address. Claire de Lune . . . Chauvinet . . . Thank you! (*Hangs up.*) You see, I'm still trying to get you a butler. (YVONNE *holds out towel for him. Starting to dry her.*) All I ever think of is you and our home! How to keep you happy!

YVONNE. You make me feel so . . . so guilty.

GEORGES. *You* feel guilty?

YVONNE. Yes. I'm sure you only rush around like this . . . go on all these business trips . . . just so you can come back and spoil me.

GEORGES. But it makes me happy, darling, to spoil you! (*Looking at watch.*) Good God! Look at the time! I must be going! (*Behind her, with towel around her.*) Of course, if I could do as I wanted . . .

YVONNE. You'd stay with me?

GEORGES. Need you ask? But I have no right to indulge my fancies!

YVONNE. You know these trips of yours to Bayeux are very embarrassing for me . . .

GEORGES. (*A bit worried.*) They are? Why?

YVONNE. Because the Latouches are always inviting you to their house and you never ask them here. Why?

GEORGES. (*Thinking fast.*) Why? Why because . . . they hate travelling! Nothing can persuade them to leave their home . . . their cat . . . their canary. Bye, dear! (*Kisses her and starts to leave.*)

YVONNE. I promised you a surprise . . .

GEORGES. (*Stops.*) Oh, yes. So you did.

YVONNE. You're not very curious, are you?

GEORGES. But I am, angel. Very curious. Only tell me quickly or I shall be late!

YVONNE. (*Sits sofa.*) Relax, darling! And be happy! Unpack your bag! You don't have to take this trip!

GEORGES. What? But I do! A business appointment is sacred! Latouche is expecting me . . . I must see him!

YVONNE. Of course, darling. And you shall see him! GEORGES. Latouche?

YVONNE. Yes.

GEORGES. Where?

YVONNE. Here!

GEORGES. *Here?*

YVONNE. Yes, darling. I didn't want your friends to think we were rude . . . so I got this wonderful idea!

GEORGES. (*Nervously.*) What wonderful idea?

YVONNE. I found the Latouches' address in your little black book. 22 New Development Road. Right?

GEORGES. (*With a wry smile.*) Yes . . . near the race track.

YVONNE. So I said to myself: "What do I have to lose? I'll send them a telegram . . ."

GEORGES. You sent a telegram to the Latouches? What did you say?

YVONNE. "Can you come to my villa in Deauville on Friday? To have you at Clair de Lune would be an unforgettable delight. Fondest regards."

GEORGES. How did you sign it?

YVONNE. Well, since I don't know them personally, I signed your name.

GEORGES. You signed *my* name? You invited . . . them . . . here?

YVONNE. Shouldn't I have?

GEORGES. Oh, you can do anything your little heart desires. (*Patting her.*) And you do. However, *you* may invite them, but *I* know them. They won't come. Nothing can get them to leave their happy home. Goodbye, dear! (*Starts to leave again.*)

YVONNE. Well, here's their answer: "Your kind invitation new link in our friendship. 'Til Friday then. Fondest regards. Latouche."

GEORGES. New link in our friendship!

YVONNE. (*Rises.*) Now wasn't that a wonderful idea?

GEORGES. Wonderful . . . most unexpected!

YVONNE. I knew you'd be pleased.

GEORGES. To think of the Latouches here . . . in my house . . . under our roof! And they'll be arriving any minute!

YVONNE. And I can keep you quietly at home. (*Puts arms around him.*) I've planned a lovely dinner for just the four of us. It will be so cozy . . .

GEORGES. (*Dying but trying.*) Very cozy!

YVONNE. And even if you must talk business, I'll make sure you're not bored.

GEORGES. I'm sure you will.

YVONNE. Now who's going to kiss his little sweetie for having such a wonderful idea?

GEORGES. (*With a sickly grin.*) Her little sweetie. (*Kisses her.*)

YVONNE. You're tickling me!

GEORGES. (*Grimly.*) But that's nothing to what I'd like to do to you!

YVONNE. (*Misunderstanding.*) Darling! (*Cuddles up to him.* INSPECTOR LEGRAND *enters.*)

INSPECTOR. Charming! A charming picture! Deauville's a pool of virtue! Married couples adore each other! The gigolos and cocottes aren't stealing a thing . . . not even each other's clients! There's nothing . . . nothing! Not the smallest scandal! . . . It's very discouraging.

YVONNE. Will you excuse me? We're expecting guests and I have to hurry and change. (*To* GEORGES.) Happy, darling?

GEORGES. Happy? I'm out of my mind!

YVONNE. I knew you would be! (*Exits hall.*)

INSPECTOR. What a delightful wife you have! Such buoyancy! Such bounce! She must be full of surprises!

GEORGES. Loaded with them! . . . God, what a spot I'm in! (*Sits chair Downstage Left and lights cigarette.*)

INSPECTOR. (*Eagerly.*) Something serious, I hope? A bad check . . . threatening letters . . . a little seduction on the backstairs?

GEORGES. No, no, nothing that could interest the police. Unless . . .

INSPECTOR. Unless what?

GEORGES. (*Looking in direction where* YVONNE *has exited.*) Unless someone decides to shoot me . . .

INSPECTOR. Who? Why? When? Where?

GEORGES. I was only joking.

INSPECTOR. Please don't raise false hopes! You see, I'm making a round of the villas to announce my coming retirement.

GEORGES. Congratulations!

INSPECTOR. What for? Peace and quiet in Deauville? You know, it would be just my luck, if I retired today, for a crime of passion to break out tomorrow, even here, in this happy household!

GEORGES. Then don't leave us, Inspector, don't leave us!

INSPECTOR. I want to go out in a blaze of glory, so please, if you have a complaint to make against anyone, don't wait until after I've gone.

GEORGES. I'll come straight to you. (*Puts out his cigarette.*)

INSPECTOR. (*Taking report from pocket and waving it for emphasis.*) Any little thing . . . doesn't matter what. I'll turn it into the biggest scandal of the year. I'll get the whole country talking about it. The Paris newspapers will give it the front page! Radio will spread it to Kingdom Come! Television will blast it to . . .

GEORGES. Believe me, Inspector . . .

(*The lush and desirable* BABETTE LATOUCHE *enters from the hall.*)

BABETTE. Hello, Georges!

GEORGES. (*Crying out.*) Oh! It's you!

BABETTE. Yes. Of course, it's me. (*About to rush to him, stops at the sight of the* INSPECTOR.) How are you, Monsieur Chauvinet?

GEORGES. (*Gasping.*) Oh . . . er . . . very well, thank you!

BABETTE. The door was open. Nobody answered when I rang.

GEORGES. The maid is out of order. I mean, I want you to meet Inspector Legrand of the Deauville Police.

BABETTE. (*Drawing back.*) Oh! Pleased to meet you.

GEORGES. Madame Babette Latouche of Bayeux . . .

INSPECTOR. The pleasure's mine, madame. I'm dazzled! Sunshine has entered the house!

BABETTE. (*Crosses to bar.*) How very flattering, Inspector!

INSPECTOR. Ah, if only I were twenty years younger!

GEORGES. She'd still be a baby!

INSPECTOR. Yes, isn't it a pity? But that's my fate. Too little, too soon or too late! Well, I must continue on my rounds.

GEORGES. Good luck!

INSPECTOR. Thanks! (*To* BABETTE.) I hope to have the pleasure of meeting you again, Madame . . . ? (*Questioningly.*) Madame . . . ?

GEORGES. Latouche!

INSPECTOR. (*Thoughtfully, again waving report.*) Latouche. Madame Latouche. Oh, no! No! It can't be. Still, you never can tell. (*Exits hall. Throughout this Scene* GEORGES *is worried his wife may appear at any moment.*)

BABETTE. (*Arms wide open to embrace him.*) Georges, darling!

GEORGES. Dear Madame Latouche . . . !

BABETTE. Madame Latouche? (*Wags head, goes into his arms.*) Don't ever call me anything but . . . Babette!

GEORGES. (*Backing away.*) Thank you, Babette. So . . . er . . . here you are!

BABETTE. (*Again in his arms.*) Your telegram was such a wonderful surprise!

GEORGES. Yes. Wasn't it? (*Escapes again.*)

BABETTE. I'm afraid I misjudged you terribly.

GEORGES. Oh. Why?

BABETTE. Because I was certain you were like all men . . . eager to have an affair as long as there are no strings attached.

GEORGES. How could you think such a thing!

BABETTE. When you came to see me, you were always in such a hurry to be off again.

GEORGES. Business, Babette, my business. It keeps me constantly on the move.

BABETTE. (*Exploring room; suspiciously.*) You never even told me where you lived. I had such horrible misgivings! Perhaps you had some serious tie! (*Crosses aggressively to him.*)

GEORGES. (*Shrugging.*) Serious tie?

BABETTE. Suppose . . . suppose you were married!

GEORGES. Married! (*Sickly laugh.*)

BABETTE. Just thinking of it would make me furious!

GEORGES. As bad as that!

BABETTE. But wasn't I being stupid! For how could any man be such a cad, such a hypocrite, as to make love to me, while he had a wife!

GEORGES. Oh, any man who would do that!

BABETTE. (*Taking both his hands.*) Forgive me. Please forgive me, darling Georges, for ever having doubted you.

GEORGES. It wasn't very nice.

BABETTE. From now on, I shall put all my trust in your strong, capable, understanding hands. (*She puts his arms around her, his hands on her bottom.*)

GEORGES. (*Breaking away.*) And as soon as you are settled . . . emotionally, that is . . . I shall join you.

BABETTE. Join me? Where?

GEORGES. At the hotel.

BABETTE. What hotel?

GEORGES. We're going to jump in my car and look for something suitable in the neighborhood. Come on. Let's go! (*Takes her hand and starts for hall.*)

BABETTE. No, Georges. Your tender consideration makes me surer than ever. I'm staying here! (*Sits sofa.*)

GEORGES. But I can't let you! I mean . . . what will people think?

BABETTE. By refusing to take advantage of this situation, you have proved to me beyond the shadow of a doubt that you are worthy of every sacrifice . . . (*Pulls him on sofa.*) Every sacrifice!

GEORGES. Now, now, Babette! It's unfair to tempt me. I'll lose my head!

BABETTE. And so shall I! Let's throw caution to the wind!

GEORGES. No, no! (*Pushing her away.*) Let me savor my happiness! I've waited so long for this moment!

BABETTE. No longer than I have!

GEORGES. (*Wailing.*) Oh, Babette!

BABETTE. And with *my* passion . . .

GEORGES. You must control your passion!

BABETTE. Not any more! (*Her arms around him.*) Thank God there's a limit to everything! Oh, Georges! (*He is on his back; she on top of him.*)

GEORGES. (*Trying to extricate himself from under.*) No, no! Let's prolong this ecstacy!

BABETTE. I'm only flesh and blood.

GEORGES. Come with me in my car . . . (*Falls on floor.*)

BABETTE. I haven't the strength to resist you . . . (*Falls on top of him.*)

GEORGES. Please! Let's go to the garage!

BABETTE. The garage? I haven't done that since High School. (*Rises, points to door Downstage Left.*) What's in there?

GEORGES. My study.

BABETTE. (*Pulling a reluctant* GEORGES *by the hand towards study.*) I'm following you, Georges! I'm following you with my eyes closed . . . wherever you may lead me! (*Hand on handle of study door.*)

GEORGES. (*As she is about to open door.*) Wait! Wait! Something may happen! Any second! Keep calm, Babette! Don't get excited! Remember, you're the only one I love . . . the only one I want! But I'm not alone here.

BABETTE. Oh?

GEORGES. A relative lives with me.

BABETTE. Your mother?

GEORGES. No . . .

BABETTE. Your sister?

GEORGES. Yes . . . no . . .

BABETTE. Yes or no?

GEORGES. No! But it's almost the same. She's nothing more than a little sister to me! But I can't hurt her feelings . . .

BABETTE. What difference can it make to her?

GEORGES. No difference. But . . . er . . . it's a matter of principle! This person, who's nothing to me now . . .

BABETTE. Now? Then she meant something to you once?

GEORGES. Just a little . . . in the beginning . . . when I marri . . . (*Hand goes up to his mouth.*)

BABETTE. (*With a cry.*) Married! You're married!

GEORGES. No . . .

BABETTE. No?

GEORGES. Well, yes . . .

BABETTE. Yes or no?

GEORGES. Yes.

BABETTE. Oh!

GEORGES. But just a little bit! . . . Everything is over between us . . . she's just like a little sister to me!

BABETTE. You cheat! And you asked me to come here!

GEORGES. Not me! My wife sent you that telegram!

BABETTE. (*Amazed.*) Your wife?

GEORGES. But you don't understand. She doesn't suspect . . . that is, I often tell her about my friends, the Latouches of Bayeux.

BABETTE. (*Out front.*) And these friends are . . . *me?*

GEORGES. Yes.

BABETTE. (*Beating his chest.*) You're as despicable as the rest!

GEORGES. Yes.

BABETTE. (*Pursuing him.*) Why didn't you tell me the truth before?

GEORGES. (*Backing away.*) I was afraid of losing you . . .

BABETTE. (*Pursuing.*) You have lost me . . . forever!

GEORGES. But you said you loved me.

BABETTE. I hate you!

GEORGES. But you loved me when you thought I was a bachelor!

BABETTE. I hate you! (*Pointing to hall.*) Get out of here!

GEORGES. (*He starts to leave; stops; returns.*) Look, you must go back to Bayeux!

BABETTE. Never! I shall never go back to Bayeux!

GEORGES. Why?

BABETTE. I have my reasons!

GEORGES. What reasons?

BABETTE. Why should I tell you?

GEORGES. You can't stay here!

BABETTE. Where shall I go?

GEORGES. I don't know!

BABETTE. Neither do I!

GEORGES. My wife will be coming in any second!

BABETTE. You'll introduce me . . .

GEORGES. How can I?

BABETTE. She invited me . . . she'll expect to see me.

GEORGES. You're alone! (*Beats hands on knees.*) *You have no husband!*

BABETTE. (*Mimics him.*) Sorry, but I forgot to bring one with me! (LEONARD *rushes in through French windows.*)

LEONARD. Here I am! (*Not noticing* BABETTE.) I've checked out of the hotel . . . everything's fixed . . . and here I am!

GEORGES. My God! I forgot about you!

LEONARD. (*Reproachfully.*) So soon? (*Seeing* BABETTE.) Oh, I beg your pardon! . . . Madame!

BABETTE. Monsieur . . .

LEONARD. I'm delighted to meet you. And I must rush to congratulate you on having found in my dear friend, Georges, that rarity among men . . . the *husband* who adores his *wife!* (*Starts to kiss her hand.*)

BABETTE. (*Pulls hand away and glares at* GEORGES.) Really?

LEONARD. The first words out of his mouth.

BABETTE. (*Crossing to* GEORGES.) He told you he adored his wife?

GEORGES. No, no, no . . .

LEONARD. Worship would be a better word! There was no stopping him once he got started: a beautiful person . . . the most delicious . . . the most delectable . . . so tasty!

BABETTE. (*To* GEORGES.) Oh-h-h!

GEORGES. Pay no attention to him! He's making it up! He's a poet!

LEONARD. I'm not making anything up! My heart is still racing! He made marriage sound like a fairy tale!

BABETTE. And I've come here to hear that!

GEORGES. (*Furiously.*) You idiot! *She's* not my wife!

LEONARD. (*Rolling under the blow.*) Oooh . . . yes . . . very nice, too. Somebody goofed.

GEORGES. Somebody certainly has.

LEONARD. Then . . . it's time you introduced us.

GEORGES. (*To* BABETTE.) This is an old school friend who, fortunately, I haven't seen for a good many years.

LEONARD. How nicely you put it!

GEORGES. Monsieur Leonard Jolijoli.

LEONARD. Jolijoli, written in one word, exactly as it's pronounced.

GEORGES. And this is Madame Babette Latouche of Bayeux.

LEONARD. (*Crossing to her and missing her extended hand.*) Oh, so you're the bitch . . .

BABETTE. What?

LEONARD. Er . . . I mean the bit of . . . er . . . the *lady from Bayeux!* And I must rush to congratulate you on having found in my dear friend, Georges, such an ardent lover!

BABETTE. (*Crossing to* GEORGES.) Because I'm the most delicious . . . the most delectable?

GEORGES. But this time it's true!

BABETTE. Really, Georges! (*Sits sofa.*)

LEONARD. I never lie . . . as a rule . . . but I must confess when I was speaking of Georges' wife . . .

GEORGES. That'll do, Leonard! That'll do! (LEONARD *shrugs.*) And since you have such a talent for goofing, I'd better tell you that Yvonne . . .

LEONARD. (*Crossing to* BABETTE.) Yvonne! What a sweet name!

GEORGES. Yvonne's my wife! And she's invited Madame Latouche and her husband here!

LEONARD. (*To* BABETTE.) But I thought you weren't married?

GEORGES. She isn't . . . that's the problem!

LEONARD. Oh, Georges! When your wife finds out, you're going to get into trouble!

GEORGES. She won't! I've got an idea! (*To* LEONARD.) You want to stay here, don't you?

LEONARD. Yes, please.

GEORGES. (*Crosses to* BABETTE.) And you, Babette, for some reason or other, insist you can't go back to Bayeux.

BABETTE. It's impossible!

GEORGES. All right, Leonard, you can stay here . . .

LEONARD. Oh, good!

GEORGES. But on one condition.

LEONARD. Yes?

GEORGES. For a few hours you're going to be Monsieur Latouche.

LEONARD. Me?

GEORGES. Yes, my good friend Latouche from Bayeux. (*To* BABETTE.) All right with you?

BABETTE. No!

GEORGES. It means as much to you as it does to me!

BABETTE. Oh, do what you want! I don't care!

LEONARD. Me? With a wife? No, thank you, I'm not into bondage!

GEORGES. Then out you go to sink or swim with Zizi!

LEONARD. That's blackmail!

GEORGES. Make up your mind!

LEONARD. (*Crosses to* BABETTE.) Madame Latouche?

BABETTE. Yes?

LEONARD. And what, if he existed, would be your husband's Christian name?

BABETTE. How about . . . Jacques?

LEONARD. Jacques is such a common name!

GEORGES. Then Jacques it is! Thank you, Babette!

BABETTE. Don't thank me. I'm not doing this for you!

LEONARD. And what, if any, would be Monsieur Latouche's vocation?

GEORGES. The same as mine. We'd be in the same business . . . handling the same products.

LEONARD. Which are?

GEORGES. Rubber heels, rubber balls, rubber gloves, rubber bands, etcetera, etcetera.

LEONARD. It's the etcetera I find most alarming. Do you expect me, France's most promising poetic dramatist, to become a travelling salesman in rubber goodies?

GEORGES. I wouldn't turn up my nose at rubber goodies if I were you!

LEONARD. Can I help it if I don't respond to rubber goodies? (*To* BABETTE.) Balloons! He expects me to sell balloons!

GEORGES. Oh, stop being such a Moumou!

BABETTE. Moumou?

GEORGES. It's his nickname. It means soft as mush.

BABETTE. (*Rises and crosses to* LEONARD.) Lovely!
From now on you're Moumou to me!

LEONARD. I am not soft as mush. I have a backbone.
I'm trapped, that's all. Georges has trapped me!

GEORGES. Well?

LEONARD. Well, all right. I'll be her husband. But
only for dinner, mind you.

GEORGES. Just make sure you don't give me away
to my wife.

LEONARD. I'll try not to. But I've never been to
Bayeux in my life! What am I supposed to know about
the place?

BABETTE. (*Sits chair Left Center.*) It has streets . . .

LEONARD. Hmm.

GEORGES. A lot of houses . . .

LEONARD. Not really?

BABETTE. Several bakery shops . . .

LEONARD. Oh.

GEORGES. A famous tapestry . . .

LEONARD. Yes, the Bayeux tapestry.

BABETTE. A street lamp on every corner . . .

LEONARD. How illuminating.

GEORGES. With a lady leaning against each one.

BABETTE. How do *you* know?

GEORGES. I . . . I . . . saw it on a postcard.
(*To* LEONARD.) A race track . . . with horses . . .

LEONARD. How unusual.

GEORGES. My God! Here comes Yvonne!

LEONARD. Yvonne? Who's that?

BABETTE. His wife! (*Frightened,* LEONARD *rushes to
window seat to escape the situation.* YVONNE *enters
from hall.* BABETTE *is seated Left Center chair.*)

GEORGES. (*Going to* YVONNE.) Our guests have just
arrived.

YVONNE. (*Crossing to* BABETTE.) So sorry I wasn't
here to receive you. But we're without a butler and I
have to attend to everything myself. (*Shaking hands
with* BABETTE.) This is such a pleasure.

BABETTE. For us, too.

YVONNE. (*Going to* LEONARD, *who is lost in thought, his back to her.*) And this is Monsieur Latouche?

GEORGES. (*Raising his voice.*) Yes, *Jacques* . . . my old friend, *Jacques Latouche!*

LEONARD. (*Jumping up.*) Oh! Yes! That's me!

YVONNE. My husband says he's never had such a good friend.

LEONARD. Yes . . . yes . . . I'm the best friend a man ever had.

YVONNE. You have both been so kind to him!

BABETTE. I only wish I could have done more!

GEORGES. So do I! I mean, I couldn't take advantage.

YVONNE. Now that you've found your way here, I hope you will come more often.

BABETTE. We'd love to . . . (*In trying to put her arm around* LEONARD, *who is standing by her chair, her hand accidentally goes between his thighs and sticks out in front of him.* GEORGES *and* YVONNE *stare at this in amazement.*) That is if Monsieur Chauvinet doesn't find our being here to disturbing.

GEORGES. (*Trying to brush it off.*) Disturbing? You?

LEONARD. And I don't have to cross the Indian Ocean . . .

YVONNE. Cross the Indian Ocean? I thought you hated traveling?

LEONARD. Me? Not at all! Why I adore it!

GEORGES. Of course you hate traveling, Jacques! You've told me a thousand times!

LEONARD. I have? Oh! . . . Yes . . . er . . . what I meant was . . . I travel a lot in my imagination . . .

YVONNE. Have you always lived in Bayeux?

LEONARD. No, thank God!

GEORGES. But of course you have . . . ever since you were a baby!

LEONARD. Oh yes. Of course. Ever since I was a baby. But when I was an unborn baby . . . we lived in Alsace Lorraine. (*Low to* BABETTE.) This is getting terrible!

YVONNE. I'm quite familiar with Bayeux . . .

LEONARD. You're lucky!

BABETTE. Pretty little place, isn't it?

LEONARD. Yes, it's a pretty little place.

GEORGES. (*Cueing him.*) So historical.

LEONARD. Oh, yes. So hysterical. Er . . . I mean historical! All those lamps posts with streets. And those women on every corner leaning against bakeries selling postcards. (*Behind* YVONNE'S *back,* GEORGES *starts to pantomime the tapestry.* LEONARD *hasn't a clue what he means.* GEORGES *tries harder . . . and harder . . . and harder.*) Oh yes . . . not to forget to mention the . . . ? the . . . ? (GEORGES *mimes tap . . . ass . . . tree.*) Of course! The tapasstree! (*Really rocking, nodding his head happily.*)

YVONNE. Of course. The Bayeux tapestry.

LEONARD. Yes, the Bayeux tapestry!

YVONNE. In what part of the city do you live?

LEONARD. (*Still nodding.*) Yes! . . . Oh. What part? what part? . . . The residential part. It's near something. (*Low to* BABETTE.) What's it near? (*Behind* YVONNE'S *back,* GEORGES *starts to imitate galloping horses. Again* LEONARD *hasn't a clue what he means.* GEORGES *tries galloping faster . . . and faster . . . and faster.*) Oh, I know! It's right near the *lunatic asylum.* (GEORGES *desperately shakes his head "no" and tries, in pantomime, to set him straight.* YVONNE *almost catches him.* GEORGES *looks innocent.*)

BABETTE. He means near the track. The race track.

LEONARD. It's the same thing. Badabum! Badabúm! Horses running like crazy! We live on a quaint old street . . .

YVONNE. (*At bar, pouring glasses of sherry.*) Old street? And it's called New Development Road?

LEONARD. Is it? I mean isn't that curious? You never know what they're going to call a street these days.

GEORGES. It's an old street with new houses.

LEONARD. Exactly. (*Despairingly.*) Oh, my God!

(*Sits sofa and grimaces dolefully at* GEORGES, *failing to notice* YVONNE *is offering him a sherry.*)

YVONNE. Monsieur Latouche, may I. . . ?

GEORGES. Jacques! (LEONARD, *not recognizing the name, takes no notice.*)

BABETTE. *Moumou* . . . Madame Chauvinet is offering you a sherry! . . . Well, take it!

LEONARD. Oh, excuse me! . . . Thank you. Thank you very much. (*Looks balefully at* BABETTE.)

GEORGES. Jacques is always with the Man in the Moon.

LEONARD. (*Rises.*) Don't I wish it! (*Low to* BABETTE, *angrily.*) Moumou!

YVONNE. You must be very busy organizing new branches.

LEONARD. Oh yes. What new branches?

GEORGES. You know . . . our products. (*Behind* YVONNE'S *back,* GEORGES *mimes blowing up and breaking balloon.*)

LEONARD. Oh yes . . . balloons! Big balloons, little balloons, long, tall, short, fat, thin balloons. Oh yes! Any old balloon that tickles your fancy! . . . Et-cetera!

GEORGES. Madame Latouche, your husband is so enthusiastic about our products, he gets carried away.

BABETTE. He should be!

GEORGES. Really, we're taking up too much of Jacques' time. (*To* BABETTE *and* LEONARD.) After dinner, I'll drive you home. (BABETTE, *unseen by* YVONNE, *makes signs to the contrary.*)

YVONNE. (*To* LEONARD.) Oh, as soon as that? You were going to keep my husband in Bayeux for the night, so I shan't let *you* go until tomorrow morning!

LEONARD. Tomorrow morning?

YVONNE. And I even hope to keep you over the weekend.

GEORGES. Really, Yvonne, we've imposed on Jacques too much already.

YVONNE. (*Putting arms tenderly around* GEORGES' *neck, much to his discomfort.*) But darling, considering how often you've been their guest, you should try and persuade them too!

BABETTE. Moumou . . . Madame Chauvinet puts her invitation so nicely we simply can't refuse! (LEONARD *wags his head "no, no, no, no!" To* GEORGES, *defiantly.*) Thank you! We're staying!

YVONNE. Wonderful! . . . Now if you'll excuse me, I'll just peek in the guest room.

GEORGES. But, Yvonne!

YVONNE. Isn't it wonderful, darling? Just we four . . . two loving couples! What fun! (*Exits hall.* LEONARD *is appalled,* BABETTE *furious and* GEORGES *rattled.*)

LEONARD. Oh, my God!

BABETTE. (*Imitating* YVONNE.) Just we four . . . two loving couples . . . what fun! (*Raging.*) Oh, the way she cuddles up to you!

GEORGES. It's just for appearance's sake, that's all!

BABETTE. Just short of violating you in public! (*Fiercely to* LEONARD.) Yes or no? (BABETTE *slaps* LEONARD *and he falls to the floor.*)

LEONARD. I don't know!

GEORGES. (*To* LEONARD.) A fine performance you turned in!

LEONARD. (*Rises.*) No wonder. You got me so confused I didn't know who I was with your badabum, badabum and your crazy gestures!

BABETTE. Any fool could tell what he meant! (*Shrugging.*) Lunatic asylum!

LEONARD. He looked more like a lunatic than a race horse!

GEORGES. Listen! Both of you! Let me find you a room in a hotel!

BABETTE. No! I'm sleeping here!

LEONARD. With me?

GEORGES. (*To* BABETTE.) Look, there's only one guest room, with only one bed.

BABETTE. Good! I'm sharing it with him to make you suffer!

LEONARD. I'm sorry but that's out!

BABETTE. Don't exasperate me, Moumou!

LEONARD. And what's more, don't call me Moumou!

BABETTE. Oh, get down to the station and bring my luggage!

GEORGES. What do you have . . . an overnight bag?

BABETTE. An overnight bag? Three large suitcases, a half dozen hat boxes . . .

GEORGES. What!

BABETTE. My golf clubs, tennis racket . . .

GEORGES. Is that all?

BABETTE. No. My skiis.

GEORGES. Skiis!

BABETTE. I came prepared for anything!

LEONARD. You do it on skiis, Georges?

BABETTE. And then, of course, there are my trunks!

GEORGES. Trunks! You're asked out to dinner and you bring your trunks?

BABETTE. I was invited out for much more than dinner! The telegram implied a long stay! I came here thinking of the future . . . of starting a new life . . . with you, Georges.

GEORGES. But that's impossible.

BABETTE. I know it is . . . and you're going to pay for it!

GEORGES. What do you mean?

BABETTE. I'm going to watch you live and get my revenge!

LEONARD. Take your revenge on him but please leave *me* out of it.

BABETTE. Oh no, Moumou! You're going to be my instrument of revenge!

LEONARD. I'll be no such thing! You can get yourself another instrument!

GEORGES. Come, come, Babette! All this talk of revenge and from such a sweet girl.

BABETTE. (*Like a tigress.*) Sweet? You've taken all the sweetness out of me!

GEORGES. Not yet . . .

BABETTE. No, I found you out just in time! I'll show you both . . .

LEONARD. Now really!

GEORGES. (*Tenderly, going to put his arms around her.*) Darling! Sweetheart!

BABETTE. Don't touch me!

LEONARD. Don't touch her, Georges! She'll go bang!

BABETTE. Go down to the station and get my luggage!

GEORGES. All right, all right, I'm going!

BABETTE. You and your little sister!

LEONARD. (*To* BABETTE, *indignantly.*) Oh, if it's one thing I'm not, it's his little sister! (*To* GEORGES.) Imagine me . . . married . . . and to her!

BABETTE. Go down to the station!

LEONARD. All right, all right, I'm going! . . . His little sister! (BABETTE *throws the nearest ornament or pillow at* GEORGES *and* LEONARD *as they hurry out.*)

CURTAIN

ACT TWO

The living room of the Villa Clair de Lune. One hour later. BABETTE, *on the sofa, is alone. She is holding an open book but her mind is elsewhere. A bearded man, burly, and with his collar turned up, enters cautiously from the garden, giving the impression he is either being followed or is hiding from someone.*

JACQUES. Babette! . . .

BABETTE. (*Startled.*) Oh! . . .

JACQUES. It's me!

BABETTE. Jacques!

JACQUES. Darling!

BABETTE. (*Furiously.*) Don't you darling me!

JACQUES. Who has a better right to *darling* you?

BABETTE. You'll never darling *me* again!

JACQUES. But Babette, I'm desperate! It's been weeks . . .

BABETTE. And it will be a good many more weeks before . . .

JACQUES. No! I can't wait!

BABETTE. Don't come near me or I'll scream!

JACQUES. What are you afraid of?

BABETTE. You may be my husband but . . .

JACQUES. Oh no, Babette! You've got this all wrong. I'm only interested in your forgiveness.

BABETTE. (*Flabbergasted.*) My forgiveness!

JACQUES. I've risked everything for that. This morning I crept back to Bayeux . . . sneaking down alleys and back streets . . . gambling my freedom. It was a close shave.

BABETTE. Not close enough. You look like an ape.

JACQUES. I can't take any chances on being recognized! (*Takes off false beard and throws it on sofa.*) When I got back to the house, you were gone!

37

BABETTE. How could I stay after what you had done!

JACQUES. I was in the depths of despair . . . then I found this telegram inviting you here! I've been watching outside . . . waiting for you to be alone.

BABETTE. Two months ago you went to the corner drugstore and left me waiting. And I'd still be waiting, if I hadn't read in the newspapers the police were after you!

JACQUES. Babette, you know I'm an honest man!

BABETTE. If you're honest, I'd hate to meet a dishonest man!

JACQUES. I lost my head . . .

BABETTE. Yes, over a call girl!

JACQUES. No! She was a retired airline hostess!

BABETTE. Who couldn't break the habit of saying "welcome aboard!"

JACQUES. But I paid for my transgression with checks to her dressmaker . . . her jeweler . . . her furrier . . .

BABETTE. And *I* couldn't even have a rabbit skin coat!

JACQUES. Oh, but you were so much in my thoughts!

BABETTE. Thank you!

JACQUES. And, of course, there was my bank account . . . about to be swallowed up. So I rushed down and drew out all my money.

BABETTE. Before the checks were paid?

JACQUES. Naturally! I wanted to try my luck at the Casino and double my money!

BABETTE. You fool! You've lost everything?

JACQUES. Yes. My checks became worthless! And faced with disgrace, prison . . . there was nothing left for me to do but disappear.

BABETTE. Which you did, leaving *me* to face the neighbors! Everybody pointing at me! It was so charming, I had to leave town!

JACQUES. I want to make it up to you, Babette. I want to start our life together over again. Only this time it will be different.

BABETTE. (*Weakening.*) Will it?

JACQUES. I'll settle down . . . keep regular hours . . become respectable.

BABETTE. Do you mean that, Jacques?

JACQUES. Every last word. I'll become an honest man again . . . (*Kisses her left hand.*) make you proud of me. (*Kisses her right hand.*) Give me your ring and I'll pawn it.

BABETTE. What!

JACQUES. I have a wonderful new system!

BABETTE. No!

JACQUES. In one night at the Casino, I can win back everything!

BABETTE. You won't get a sou from me!

JACQUES. But the police are after me! How can I get a job with the name Jacques Latouche on my Identity Card?

BABETTE. That's your problem! I'm through with you!

JACQUES. (*Grabs her wrist.*) I'll never give you up! I love you!

BABETTE. A fine proof of your love I've had!

JACQUES. A moment of madness!

BABETTE. Huh! Perhaps I'll have a moment of madness, too.

JACQUES. If I ever catch you with another man . . . (*Suspiciously.*) What are you doing in this house? Who are you staying with?

BABETTE. Friends.

JACQUES. *Monsieur* Chauvinet?

BABETTE. And his *wife!* And since they're not from Bayeux, they know nothing of you or your bad reputation . . . so get out of here!

JACQUES. Not until I see *Madame* Chauvinet!

BABETTE. Get out of here! I never want to see you again! Never! Never! Never!

JACQUES. Where do you want me to go?

BABETTE. You can go straight to . . .

JACQUES. (*Picks up beard and puts it on.*) Quiet! Someone's coming!

YVONNE. (*She enters from dining room.*) Monsieur . . .

JACQUES. (*Uneasily.*) Madame!

YVONNE. (*After a short pause, to* BABETTE.) Do you know this gentleman?

BABETTE. Me? No!

YVONNE. What do you want, monsieur?

JACQUES. Nothing, madame.

YVONNE. Nothing?

JACQUES. No, nothing at all.

YVONNE. Do you want to see my husband?

JACQUES. Er . . . yes . . . but I didn't want to disturb you.

YVONNE. I am Madame Chauvinet.

JACQUES. Oh, yes . . . Chauvinet . . . Villa Clair de Lune . . . Deauville.

YVONNE. That's right.

JACQUES. That's what the telegram said.

YVONNE. Telegram! Oh, then the agency sent you.

JACQUES. Oh, yes. *Yes!* The agency sent me!

YVONNE. Why didn't you say so?

JACQUES. I thought you knew.

YVONNE. Well, what we need is a butler-valet . . .

JACQUES. I'm fully qualified!

YVONNE. You must be if the agency sent you. The position's yours, if you want it.

JACQUES. Want it? To stay here . . . in this house! (*Looking at* BABETTE.) That would suit me perfectly, madame!

YVONNE. But first I ought to tell you, you won't have much free time.

JACQUES. I don't even want my day off.

YVONNE. No? Why?

JACQUES. Because . . . because I'm family orientated. When I find a home, I make it a home. I never want to leave it.

BABETTE. Hah!

YVONNE. (*To* BABETTE.) Did you say something?

BABETTE. The sentiment. I'm all choked up.

JACQUES. Besides, Deauville's so crowded. I don't like crowds. I wouldn't be surprised if I never left the house!

YVONNE. All the same, this isn't a prison!

JACQUES. I should hope not, madame!

YVONNE. Well, as you wish. (*To* BABETTE.) You've brought me luck, Madame Latouche! You arrive and I find a butler!

BABETTE. What a happy coincidence! (*Behind* YVONNE's *back, she gives vent to her anger.*)

YVONNE. (*To* JACQUES.) My husband will speak to you about your wages. Now when can you start?

JACQUES. Immediately.

YVONNE. That's fine. If you'll walk this way . . .

JACQUES. (*Watching her walk.*) Walk *that* way?

YVONNE. Yes. (JACQUES *mimics her walk.*) The kitchen is through here . . . the maid will acquaint you with our routine.

JACQUES. Very good, madame . . . At your service, madame . . . I am delighted, madame . . .

YVONNE. All right, all right . . . (JACQUES *exits dining room.*)

BABETTE. Aren't you afraid to engage a butler without first asking for his references?

YVONNE. Ask for his references? I'm lucky enough to find one these days!

BABETTE. But he's so . . . strange.

YVONNE. Yes, but so home-loving. He should make some woman a splendid husband.

BABETTE. Just splendid. (CLAUDINE *enters from the hall, outrageously dressed in the very latest fashion.*) Madame, you have a visitor.

YVONNE. Oh? (*Turns, then casually.*) No . . . just my maid.

CLAUDINE. Oh, madame . . .

YVONNE. Claudine, will you be kind enough to put on your uniform?

CLAUDINE. With pleasure, madame.

YVONNE. And get the blue room ready for our guests, Monsieur and Madame Latouche . . .

CLAUDINE. (*Amazed, almost shouting.*) . . . of Bayeux?

YVONNE. Of Bayeux.

CLAUDINE. Whoever would have thought it!

YVONNE. Now will you kindly attend to your duties!

CLAUDINE. Yes, madame. I'll attend to *my* duties . . . (*Looking at* BABETTE.) although I know certain women who attend to duties that *don't* belong to them! (*Exits dining room.*)

YVONNE. Whatever can she mean by that?

BABETTE. I wonder!

YVONNE. But that's the kind of servant you find in Deauville these days! (*Laughing.*) However! She might not suit me but she may suit the new butler.

BABETTE. I'm sure she will.

(*Offstage* CLAUDINE *squeals.* BABETTE *and* YVONNE *nod to each other.* GEORGES *and* LEONARD *enter from the hall loaded down with suitcases, tennis racket, skiis, golf clubs, etc.*)

LEONARD. I'm the advance guard . . . and oh me, oh my, am I exhausted!

GEORGES. (*To* BABETTE, *with a wan smile.*) The rest is coming by truck . . . a large truck.

YVONNE. Leave it there. I'll ring for the butler. (*Presses button.*)

GEORGES. Butler?

YVONNE. Yes, darling. The agency just sent us one.

GEORGES. Well, at least *that's* something. (*To* BA-

BETTE.) I mean, having a butler will make your stay more pleasant.

BABETTE. Oh, yes. Indeed *he* will! (JACQUES *enters from dining room wearing butler's white jacket.*)

YVONNE. Will you take this bit of luggage upstairs to the guest room . . . and put yourself at the disposal of Monsieur and Madame Latouche?

JACQUES. What?

GEORGES. Yes . . . of Monsieur and Madame Latouche.

JACQUES. (*Looking at* LEONARD.) This is Madame Latouche's husband? (BABETTE, *seated in armchair Left Center, laughs wickedly and gleefully crosses her legs. Staring angrily at her.*) Ohhh!!! (BABETTE *grins back at him.*)

GEORGES. There's no doubt about it!

LEONARD. Certainly not! I'm that lady's husband.

JACQUES. Are you sure, m'sieur?

LEONARD. (*Emphatically.*) Of course! I am Jacques Latouche of Bayeux!

BABETTE. Yes . . . of course he is!

LEONARD. I don't see why that should surprise you . . . (JACQUES *slaps suitcase and growls at* LEONARD, *who jumps.*) Oh! For heaven's sake! (*To* BABETTE.) After you, darling!

BABETTE. Thank you, sweetheart. (*Hits* JACQUES *on chest, brushing him aside, and exits hall.*)

LEONARD. Oh, that beard! (*Exits hall.*)

JACQUES. (*Following close behind, loaded with luggage; menacingly.*) I'm close behind you, Monsieur Latouche! (*Exits hall.*)

GEORGES. God, he's peculiar!

YVONNE. Your friend Latouche? He certainly is!

GEORGES. No, I mean the butler . . .

YVONNE. Georges, how did you come to pick a friend like Monsieur Latouche?

GEORGES. Common interests . . .

YVONNE. (*Raising her eyebrows.*) *Common in-*

terests? . . . Or could it be the interest you have in common in the same woman?

GEORGES. I don't understand.

YVONNE. Georges, you told me Madame Latouche was an insignificant mousey woman . . . and I find this beautiful, vivacious, flamboyant creature.

GEORGES. She's changed.

YVONNE. Since last week?

GEORGES. (*Thinking fast.*) It must be . . . the excitement of taking a trip . . . with her husband . . . at last.

YVONNE. And it isn't on *her* account that you've been going to Bayeux so often?

GEORGES. Don't be ridiculous, darling!

YVONNE. Am I being ridiculous?

GEORGES. My silly darling! Let me kiss your sweet lips and stop them from saying these silly, silly things! (*Kisses her.*)

YVONNE. (*Coyly.*) More. (*A long kiss.* LEONARD *enters from hall and watches unabashedly.*) More! (*Another kiss.* LEONARD *exits hall and returns immediately with a hand bell. He shakes it and the clapper drops off. There hasn't been a sound from the bell.* LEONARD *is perplexed. He doesn't know how to announce his presence. The kiss goes on. Finally he gets an idea.*)

LEONARD. (*Shaking the bell.*) Ding-a-ling-a-ling! (GEORGES *and* YVONNE *spring apart. They notice* LEONARD'S *dilemma with the bell and start to laugh. It's infectious, going from one actor to the other, until they have to turn away from the audience to try and control their laughter. It's hopeless. The audience has joined in, laughing at the actors' predicament.*)

GEORGES. (*Fighting to control his laughter.*) Well . . . don't just stand there. For God's sake, say something!

LEONARD. May I come in? (*They burst out laughing again.* GEORGES *picks up the clapper from the floor.*)

GEORGES. (*To* LEONARD.) You dropped your little dinger! (*More laughter, but they get it under control and the play proceeds. To* LEONARD.) Oh! It's only you, Jacques!

YVONNE. Who did you expect?

GEORGES. No one, dear. No one at all.

LEONARD. Ah, madame, I must congratulate you again on having such an ardent lover!

YVONNE. Lover?

GEORGES. He means husband!

LEONARD. What? . . . Oh yes, of course. You're his wife.

YVONNE. You'd forgotten?

GEORGES. (*Slapping* LEONARD *hard on the back.*) Good old Jacques! Always thinking about our business!

LEONARD. Oh, yes! . . . And what a business!

YVONNE. I'll leave you together while I see if Madame Latouche has everything she needs. (*Exits hall.*)

GEORGES. My God, Leonard, you have to be more careful! You don't seem to know whether you're talking to Yvonne or Babette!

LEONARD. A woman's a woman. They just don't register.

GEORGES. You have a short in your detector.

LEONARD. Besides, I'm all upset!

GEORGES. Why?

LEONARD. Well, that *butler!* The way he stares at me! It's so unnerving!

GEORGES. Stare right back at him!

LEONARD. Oh, I couldn't do that! He might get the wrong idea. He gives me the shivers! And that Babette of yours . . . she gives me the shivers, too!

GEORGES. Really, Leonard . . .

LEONARD. Well, she does! And under no circumstances am I going to share a bed with a woman of the opposite sex . . .

GEORGES. You won't share a bed . . . ?

LEONARD. (*Straightening* GEORGES *out.*) With a woman of the opposite sex I know nothing about. *You* have a *twisted* mind!

GEORGES. Well, at least we agree on one thing. Babette *must* sleep alone.

LEONARD. But where shall I sleep?

GEORGES. There's a hammock in the garden!

LEONARD. Oh? And what about the morning dew? I'm very delicate . . . and susceptible to post nasal drip!

GEORGES. We have three bedrooms. The one we gave you. Yvonne's room. And mine.

LEONARD. Then you and Yvonne are no longer . . .

GEORGES. Separate rooms don't necessarily mean separate hearts.

LEONARD. They don't?

GEORGES. No, these separations are like bellows . . . (*Fanning his hand, which is on a level with his waist, back and forth, back and forth.*) fanning the flame of married love. .

LEONARD. Well, there's no point waiting until the house burns down! So tonight, why don't you and Yvonne . . .

GEORGES. No!

LEONARD. Oh.

GEORGES. However, there's this room with a couch you can use.

LEONARD. Oh, good!

GEORGES. Oh, damn! The lights are not working. We haven't been able to get an electrician.

LEONARD. But I'm afraid of the dark . . .

GEORGES. Then back you go to Babette . . .

LEONARD. No, no! I'm not that afraid of the dark! I prefer to sleep alone no matter what!

CLAUDINE. (*In uniform, she enters.*) Monsieur Chauvinet?

GEORGES. Yes? What is it?

CLAUDINE. I take it I can now unpack your bag?

GEORGES. (*Irritably.*) It won't unpack itself.

CLAUDINE. I thought you wouldn't be going to Bayeux now that Monsieur Latouche has surprised us by coming here. (*Going up to* LEONARD, *provocatively.*) We were all so curious to know you, m'sieur.

LEONARD. Oh?

GEORGES. Claudine, you're wasting your time!

LEONARD. Well, really! (JACQUES *enters from hall.*) Oh, oh . . . here comes hairy!

JACQUES. (*To* GEORGES.) Excuse me, m'sieur. I came for the rest of the luggage.

GEORGES. All right, go ahead.

JACQUES. (*Crossing in front of* LEONARD.) Excuse me, Monsieur Latouche . . . (*Pushes him.*)

LEONARD. Yes, go right ahead. Don't let me stop you.

JACQUES. (*Turns suddenly and glowers at* LEONARD.) Are you *sure* you're Monsieur Latouche of Bayeux?

LEONARD. (*Shouting.*) Once and for all, I am! (JACQUES *stamps his foot and* LEONARD *flees.*) Come on, Georges, let's go water the peonies!

GEORGES. We have to dress for dinner.

LEONARD. I can't stand the sight of that man! . . . That beard! It looks like black shredded wheat! (JACQUES *stomps and growls after* LEONARD, *as he and* GEORGES *exit hall.*)

CLAUDINE. (*Crossing to telephone.*) Do you know who *he* is?

JACQUES. Of course. Didn't you hear him tell me?

CLAUDINE. (*Into phone.*) Deauville **666** . . . (*To* JACQUES.) He's going to become famous.

JACQUES. Jacques Latouche?

CLAUDINE. Thanks to me!

JACQUES. Why?

CLAUDINE. He's a swindler! (*Into phone.*) Hello? . . . Police Department? May I speak to Inspector Legrand?

JACQUES. (*Alarmed.*) You . . . you're calling the police?

CLAUDINE. Certainly!

JACQUES. About Monsieur Latouche?

CLAUDINE. To put him in jail! This is going to be fun!

JACQUES. (*Morosely.*) Lots of fun.

CLAUDINE. (*Into phone.*) Hello, is that you, my sweet little Inspector? . . . It's Claudine Amour. You have to come back here at once! . . . I have something hot for you. It's what you've been after! . . . What's your being twenty years younger got to do with it? I've got *Jacques Latouche* right here in the villa! . . . Yes, the swindler! Hurry over! (*Hangs up.*)

JACQUES. (*Pointing to hall where* LEONARD *exited.*) You're going to have him . . . Latouche . . . arrested?

CLAUDINE. Well, certainly! You won't tell him, will you?

JACQUES. No fear . . . because if he ever knew my name . . .

CLAUDINE. What *is* your name?

JACQUES. Me?

CLAUDINE. Yes, you. What do your friends call you?

JACQUES. My friends call me sonova . . .

CLAUDINE. Yes, but what's your name?

JACQUES. (*Trapped.*) Well . . . it's . . .

CLAUDINE. Leonard? . . . Leonard Jolijoli?

JACQUES. Huh? . . . Yes . . . Why not? I mean, how did you guess?

CLAUDINE. Because I've already found a note addressed to you in the letter box.

JACQUES. A note for me?

CLAUDINE. Yes . . . with your wallet.

JACQUES. My wallet? (*Takes wallet and note; tears open envelope.*)

CLAUDINE. With your Identity Card, too!

JACQUES. Well, I'll be damned!

CLAUDINE. And some poems . . . beautiful poems! You shouldn't have to be a butler.

JACQUES. Thank you. (*Reading note.*) "Dear Cornucopia . . ." Cornucopia?

CLAUDINE. The horn of plenty.

JACQUES. That's me! (*Reading note.*) "Dear Horny: You told me you were going to stay at Clair de Lune so I'm sending back your wallet and poems. I'm only keeping the money." The thief! And it's signed: "Your swimming instructor, Zizi."

CLAUDINE. ·You left your wallet on the beach?

JACQUES. I must have! (*Taking out contents from wallet, scans them.*) Leonard Jolijoli . . . Identity Card . . .

CLAUDINE. Yours?

JACQUES. Of course, it's mine! I was wondering what I'd do if anybody asked me for it!

CLAUDINE. But he's taken all your money . . .

JACQUES. Yes . . . it's too bad. And just when I wanted to go to the Casino.

CLAUDINE. (*Decisively.*) I'm going to do something for you! I know a reporter . . .

JACQUES. No! I don't want my name in the papers!

CLAUDINE. But a grande courtesan must encourage the Arts . . . and you've come just in time. The Normandie Sun is running a poetry contest. The grand prize is five thousand francs. (*Holding up pages of* LEONARD'S *poems.*) Tomorrow you'll be famous!

JACQUES. (*Catching hold of pages.*) No! I won't allow it!

CLAUDINE. (*Struggling to keep pages.*) But you must!

JACQUES. (*Reconsidering.*) Unless you can advance me some of the prize money . . .

CLAUDINE. (*Caressing his beard.*) A mere bagatelle, my Victor Hugo . . . (BABETTE *enters from hall.*) I'll give you the advance!

JACQUES. Wonderful!

BABETTE. Claudine! Madame Chauvinet would like to see you!

CLAUDINE. Show her in! . . . I mean, very well, madame! (*Exits hall.*)

BABETTE. You don't waste much time, do you?

JACQUES. And what about you? Who is this snake?

BABETTE. What snake?

JACQUES. Your husband!

BABETTE. *My* husband? The lowest snake that ever crawled!

JACQUES. No, not me! The snake who's fouling up my Garden of Eden! Is he your lover?

BABETTE. That's no concern of yours!

JACQUES. All right . . . I'll strangle him!

BABETTE. Don't be an idiot! Murder is serious!

JACQUES. So is infidelity . . . on the wife's part!

BABETTE. Come over here. Closer. (*Confidentially.*) He's a private detective.

JACQUES. Him?

BABETTE. Hired by a firm you gave a bad check to.

JACQUES. But that's no reason for him to be living here as your husband!

BABETTE. He threatened to have me arrested as your accomplice. I had to say he was Monsieur Latouche.

JACQUES. What else does he expect you to do for him?

BABETTE. Really, Jacques! . . . He knew you'd come after me.

JACQUES. So, he's planning to get me arrested, is he? Well, we'll see who sleeps in jail tonight!

BABETTE. What's that?

JACQUES. Watch out! Someone's . . . (GEORGES *enters from hall.*)

BABETTE. (*To* JACQUES.) I do wish you'd take care of the rest of my luggage!

JACQUES. Yes, madame.

GEORGES. Haven't you finished with those bags? What's taking you so long?

JACQUES. It's because I'm very careful . . . very orderly. A place for everything; everything in its place. (*Drops bag.*)

GEORGES. All right, but hurry.

JACQUES. For every man there's a woman; for every woman there's a man. That's so nobody should get greedy! (*Exits hall.*)

GEORGES. He's a man of sound principles.

BABETTE. You could profit by them . . . you with your two women for one man standard!

GEORGES. Babette, you know I love only you! Desire only you!

BABETTE. I'll never forgive you for leading me on!

GEORGES. Is it my fault I met you too late?

BABETTE. You shouldn't have raised my hopes!

GEORGES. Why won't you believe I'm sincere?

BABETTE. I wish I could. I'm so helpless. But your wife is much too beautiful for me to have any illusions!

GEORGES. Time passes . . . and a frigid beauty . . .

BABETTE. (*Skeptically.*) Frigid? I don't believe it.

GEORGES. The proof is we have separate rooms.

BABETTE. Oh, that.

GEORGES. It's the best solution. Not even one more for old times' sake . . .

BABETTE. (*Willing to be persuaded.*) Oh, if only I could believe you've broken the habit!

GEORGES. Tonight Leonard will sleep alone . . . and I will come to you!

BABETTE. No, no! I won't hear of it!

GEORGES. You know you want to!

BABETTE. If only I could trust you! Start a new life with you!

GEORGES. Tonight our happiness begins!

BABETTE. You give me your word your wife means nothing to you?

GEORGES. Nothing!

BABETTE. If I find out you're lying . . . !

GEORGES. You won't! (*Holding her in his arms; cheek to cheek.*) Tomorrow I'll find you a beautiful villa in the neighborhood! Tomorrow I'll devote myself to making *you* happy! Tomorrow . . . (YVONNE *enters from hall. Waltzes out of* BABETTE'S *arms and goes to his wife.*) Tomorrow we might go out to lunch at that new restaurant. What do you think, Yvonne?

YVONNE. It's a lovely idea. But before thinking about lunch tomorrow, don't you think you ought to see about the wine for dinner tonight?

GEORGES. You're right! (*Looks uneasily from* YVONNE *to* BABETTE, *not wanting to leave them alone together.*) Absolutely right! (*Makes no move to go.*)

YVONNE. Well then?

GEORGES. But . . . aren't you coming with me?

YVONNE. And leave Madame Latouche by herself?

GEORGES. No, I don't suppose you could do that.

YVONNE. We want to chat . . . become better acquainted.

GEORGES. I'm sure you do. (*Doesn't move.*)

BABETTE. Well?

GEORGES. Well, I'd be in the way, wouldn't I? . . . Yes? Yes? (BABETTE *and* YVONNE *nod.*) Yes! (*Exits dining room.*)

YVONNE. Dear Madame Latouche, I know we hardly know each other, but may I speak to you like an old friend?

BABETTE. An old friend?

YVONNE. You see, I feel women . . . I mean married women . . . who have no reason to hurt each other . . . should, on the contrary, try to help each other.

BABETTE. (*Cautiously.*) Yes. Why not?

YVONNE. May I be frank with you?

BABETTE. Yes. Of course.

YVONNE. Somehow I've got the impression your husband doesn't give you much . . . affection.

BABETTE. He's shy.

YVONNE. And I'm not satisfied with mine, either!

BABETTE. (*Hopefully.*) Oh, no? . . . You mean everything of . . . that sort . . . is over between you and Monsieur Chauvinet?

YVONNE. Oh, that would be going much too far!

BABETTE. (*Disappointed.*) Oh! Then you're not just like a little sister to him?

YVONNE. Whatever gave you that idea! My husband is still my lover.

BABETTE. How *nice* for you.

YVONNE. And he proves it quite often.

BABETTE. (*Piqued.*) I'm glad to hear it!

YVONNE. But it seems to me the spark . . . the pre-marital spark is missing.

BABETTE. Well . . . how can *I* help?

YVONNE. Well, let's look at it this way. In cold weather even a good car may be difficult to start up . . . but, if you put a few drops of oil in the cylinder, the motor starts purring again. Well, what I have in mind is for you and I to play the part of those drops of oil . . . for our mutual benefit!

BABETTE. Become a pair of pre-marital spark plugs, as it were.

YVONNE. Exactly! I'll do a bit of flirting with your husband while you do the same with mine.

BABETTE. Just enough to start up the motor!

YVONNE. That's it! (LEONARD *enters from garden looking very dejected.*) Your husband . . . so if it's all right with you . . .

BABETTE. Go right ahead! Rev him up!

YVONNE. Ah, Monsieur Latouche . . . been keeping yourself company in the garden?

LEONARD. I was dreaming . . .

YVONNE. Of what?

LEONARD. Sailors going down to the sea in slips.

BABETTE. Ships!

YVONNE. Melancholy? And yet what a fortunate man you are!

LEONARD. (*Plaintively.*) Yes . . .

YVONNE. You have a charming wife . . .

LEONARD. (*Looks at* BABETTE, *then without enthusiasm.*) Yes . . .

BABETTE. You have a way of saying "yes" . . . my dear Moumou!

LEONARD. Don't call me Moumou! (*To* YVONNE.) Something snaps when she calls me Moumou!

BABETTE. (*Aside.*) His garter belt!

(*Throughout the following Scene,* YVONNE *pursues* LEONARD, *backing him into a corner of the sofa and eventually sprawling over him, her face close to his.*)

YVONNE. Oh, you men, you're all alike! You must always have something new! Women . . . and more women . . . and other men's women . . .

LEONARD. Oh, you're exaggerating!

YVONNE. Don't be so modest! I know what the lure of the unknown is like.

LEONARD. Really?

YVONNE. (*Looking into his eyes.*) That's why your being here excites me so!

LEONARD. (*Snatches pillow and puts it defensively between his legs.*) That's nice!

YVONNE. (*Close to* LEONARD.) Do you like to swim?

LEONARD. Well . . . er . . . I get a bit chilly. (*Slaps both sides of pillow and one corner shoots up.*)

YVONNE. (*Taking pillow from his lap.*) Are you a good swimmer?

LEONARD. No! No! I sink!

YVONNE. Well, tomorrow I'll teach you how to stay on top! (*Throws pillow away.*)

LEONARD. Oh, no, no, no! Please don't bother. Thank you very much, but no!

YVONNE. Are you afraid of me?

LEONARD. Well, no. It's not that. It's just that I've

developed an instinctive distrust of swimming instructors.

YVONNE. But it will be different with me! You'll see!

LEONARD. Why? Don't you like poetry? (JACQUES *enters from dining room.*)

JACQUES. Excuse me, madame . . . where is the silver?

YVONNE. (*On top of* LEONARD *and without turning to look at* JACQUES.) Ask Claudine.

JACQUES. She can't be disturbed. She's doing her yoga.

YVONNE. Doing her yoga?

JACQUES. Yes, madame. She's double-jointed.

YVONNE. Oh, that girl! (*Rises, to* BABETTE.) Will you excuse me?

BABETTE. Why, of course!

YVONNE. (*Cupping and caressing* LEONARD'S *face, which is on the arm of the sofa.*) I'll be back in a moment, dear Monsieur Latouche! (*Exits dining room.*)

LEONARD. What's the matter with her? (*Turns his head, coming face to face with* JACQUES, *who is peering at him. He screams.*) Ohh!!! (JACQUES *exits into dining room.*) And what did *I* ever do to him? (BABETTE *laughs.*) Stop that! If you're my wife, you ought to protect me!

BABETTE. Against whom?

LEONARD. That woman! Didn't you see? She was crawling all over me!

BABETTE. Was she really crawling all over you?

LEONARD. On her tum tum! I was being molested! And you . . . my wife . . . didn't even lift a finger to help me.

BABETTE. (*Giving vent to her pent up anger.*) I didn't lift a finger because I've had it up to here with men! They make me sick! Do you hear? Sick!

LEONARD. Now calm down . . . please! I'm upset enough already!

BABETTE. (*Advancing on him as though he were the culprit.*) One makes me believe he's a bachelor . . . then tells me he's married! Married to little sister! Well, she looks good to me, little sister with her oil in her motor!

LEONARD. What are you raving about?

BABETTE. The other one gets diddled by an airline hostess!

LEONARD. In the cockpit?

BABETTE. And he dares to threaten *me!*

LEONARD. Are you running a fever?

BABETTE. I could go mad over the first man who comes along . . . over *any* man . . . (*Stops short and stares at* LEONARD.) Come over here. Come on . . . Moumou. (LEONARD *obeys as though hypnotized.*)

LEONARD. You're giving me the shivers again . . .

BABETTE. At first sight, you're nothing to get excited about. But on closer inspection, you do have a little bit of something . . .

LEONARD. I'll thank you to leave my little bit of something out of this . . .

BABETTE. For two months I've been looking forward to this . . . and that's quite a strain on a passion like mine! (BABETTE *is standing close to* LEONARD *and they are both swaying.*)

LEONARD. You're making me seasick! . . . You know a nice, long ride on a bicycle would do you good.

BABETTE. What a waste of motion! I want to pedal with you, Moumou.

LEONARD. You want to pedal with me! All right, tomorrow morning . . .

BABETTE. No. Tonight.

LEONARD. Tonight?

BABETTE. Yes, tonight.

LEONARD. But I have no light on my bicycle! Besides I'm not your husband . . . nor your lover either.

BABETTE. But you could be! (*Puts arms around his neck.*) You could be, Moumou!

JACQUES. (*He enters from dining room.*) Madame Latouche!

LEONARD. (*Extricating himself, happily.*) Oh! What a beautiful beard!

JACQUES. (*After a piercing glance at* LEONARD.) Madame Chauvinet has asked me to announce dinner is about to be served! (*Sinisterly.*) In there . . . in there . . . Monsieur Latouche!

LEONARD. (*Frightened.*) All right . . . I'm going . . . I'm going . . .

GEORGES. (*He enters.*) Where are you going?

LEONARD. To dinner . . . I think.

GEORGES. Good idea. Are you coming, *dear* Babette?

BABETTE. Yes, certainly. (*Crossing to* LEONARD.) Jacques?

JACQUES. Yes?

BABETTE. I was talking to Jacques, my husband!

JACQUES. Oh! Excuse me!

BABETTE. Give me your arm, darling.

LEONARD. All right . . . (*Puts hand on hip.*) Well, take it!

GEORGES. (*To* BABETTE *and* LEONARD.) After you!

BABETTE. Thank you. (*To* LEONARD, *leaning on his arm.*) Jacques, darling, I feel like we're just starting on our honeymoon!

LEONARD. Oh, mercy me! (BABETTE *pushes him out the door.*) I mean . . . me too! (*Exits dining room.*)

GEORGES. I'll join you in a moment. (*To* JACQUES.) Tell me, my good man . . .

JACQUES. Yes, m'sieur?

GEORGES. First of all, what's your Christian name?

JACQUES. My Christian name? . . . er . . . (*After reflection.*) Leonard.

GEORGES. Leonard? That's odd!

JACQUES. May I ask why, m'sieur?

GEORGES. It's nothing . . . merely a coincidence.

Well, Leonard . . . (*Confidentially.*) How would you like to earn an extra five hundred francs?

JACQUES. (*Eagerly.*) Five hundred francs?

GEORGES. (*Opening his wallet.*) Of course, you've only been in my employ since this evening, but I suppose I can count on your discretion?

JACQUES. Absolutely, m'sieur . . . (*Taking money.*) Thank you, m'sieur.

GEORGES. It's a bit awkward for me to have to ask you to do this, but . . . as man to man . . . I need you! . . . Oh, it's very embarrassing . . . (*Crosses away from* JACQUES.)

JACQUES. Go ahead, m'sieur!

GEORGES. No . . . really . . .

JACQUES. Please, m'sieur!

GEORGES. Well, it's a bit sticky . . .

JACQUES. As man to man!

GEORGES. (*Crosses back to* JACQUES.) Well, here goes! I'd like to spend the night with my guest!

JACQUES. With Madame Latouche of Bayeux?

GEORGES. Yes . . . and I want you to help me.

JACQUES. Me? . . . Help you spend the night with her?

GEORGES. That's it.

JACQUES. But what about her husband?

GEORGES. Her husband? (*Poking* JACQUES.) Poor old Jacques!

JACQUES. (*Poking* GEORGES *hard.*) Yes . . . poor old Jacques!

GEORGES. He'll never know what happened!

JACQUES. That's what you think!

GEORGES. We'll fix it together so he doesn't!

JACQUES. Yes . . . of course . . . (*Laughing.*) We'll fix it together!

GEORGES. (*Laughing.*) Jacques, Jacques, poor old Jacques! (*They are both laughing away. Then* GEORGES *suddenly turns serious.*) Only there's my wife! That's a problem! We have separate rooms. She never comes into mine, but sometimes she opens the door and peeks in to see if I've fallen asleep.

JACQUES. Then I suggest you forget the whole idea!

GEORGES. That's out of the question!

JACQUES. But you don't want to risk your wife catching you out of bed!

GEORGES. But she won't catch me! You're going to take my place in bed! You'll hide your head under the pillow and if my wife does look in, she'll think it's me.

JACQUES. You have it all figured out.

GEORGES. I certainly do! Now you know what you have to do?

JACQUES. Yes, m'sieur. I know. (*Aside.*) Five hundred francs for my wife! God, I hope I hate myself in the morning!

YVONNE. (*She enters from dining room.*) Darling, what's been keeping you?

GEORGES. Nothing, nothing! I was just coming . . .

YVONNE. We're waiting to start dinner.

GEORGES. After you, my love!

YVONNE. You go in, darling . . . (*Looking at* JACQUES.) I want a word with . . .

GEORGES. With Leonard.

YVONNE. Oh, yes. Leonard.

GEORGES. Your little hubbie adores you . . . (*Blows her a kiss as he exits dining room.*)

YVONNE. Leonard, where have you served before?

JACQUES. In the army.

YVONNE. You forgot to put out the fish knives *and* the dessert spoons *and* the wine glasses . . .

JACQUES. I'm sorry, madame. But I'm worried about my wife.

YVONNE. Well, try and forget your personal problems until after dinner!

JACQUES. (*Stopping her, as she is about to leave.*) Madame! . . . If madame will permit me, I'd like to give madame proof of my devotion.

YVONNE. Yes?

JACQUES. I should be embarrassed if you made a mistake and got into bed with me tonight!

YVONNE. What!?

JACQUES. Monsieur Chauvinet has given me five hundred francs to take his place in his bed tonight.

YVONNE. Will you say that again?

JACQUES. Monsieur Chauvinet has given me five hundred francs . . .

YVONNE. All right. I heard correctly.

JACQUES. I don't wish to insinuate that monsieur might profit from this substitution by going elsewhere to sleep . . . By no means!

YVONNE. Oh no, no, nc. He would never do that.

JACQUES. But, of course, you never can tell. And there's nothing to stop madame from keeping an eye on him . . .

YVONNE. But I trust him implicitly.

JACQUES. Then I'm talking out of turn.

YVONNE. No! Please go on.

JACQUES. Well, since there's another woman in the house . . . Madame Latouche . . . No, I shouldn't say that, should I? But I *do* want to spare madame any unpleasantness.

YVONNE. Thank you, Leonard. And shall we forget what you've just told me?

JACQUES. As you wish, madame.

YVONNE. Will you serve dinner now?

JACQUES. Yes, madame . . . (*Aside.*) It always pays to do someone a good turn. (*Bumping into* LEONARD *entering from dining room.*) Are you looking for something, Monsieur Latouche?

LEONARD. (*Unpleasantly surprised.*) My case . . . I have to take my medicine . . . and I don't need your help!

JACQUES. That's too bad . . . Monsieur Latouche! (*Exits dining room.*)

LEONARD. (*Going for case on bar.*) Oh! That man! . . . It's a pill I have to take before every meal. I get dizzy spells . . . from my sympathetic nerve. Will you excuse me?

YVONNE. Of course.

LEONARD. Otherwise˙ I'll have insomnia. (*Opens case.*)

YVONNE. I do hope you'll sleep well here.

LEONARD. Me too. Georges has promised me the small room.

YVONNE. Oh, has he? Then you're not going to spend the night with Madame Latouche?

LEONARD. Oh! No! My insomnia gets on her nerves, too!

YVONNE. You're sure my husband offered you this other room?

LEONARD. Of course I'm sure.

YVONNE. Monsieur Latouche?

LEONARD. Yes?

YVONNE. I think I ought to warn you, we're both about to be deceived.

LEONARD. (*Indifferently.*) Oh? . . . (*Looking into case.*) Oh! My little box has been crushed! (*Takes pill box from case.*)

YVONNE. Did you hear what I said?

LEONARD. Yes. Why?

YVONNE. I said your wife is about to become my husband's mistress!

LEONARD. You think so? (*Swallows pill.*)

YVONNE. Is that all the impression it makes on you?

LEONARD. I have a principle in life: When anything ruffles me, I spare myself by not thinking about it. You should try it.

YVONNE. Oh, you're incredible! (*Slowly, as though to an idiot.*) My husband is paying the butler to sleep in his bed so he can join your wife!

LEONARD. Whoever would believe such a mix-up! (*Swallows water; sits bar stool.*)

YVONNE. Well, what are you going to do about it?

LEONARD. I don't know. We'll see about it tomorrow.

YVONNE. Tomorrow? Won't that be a little too late?

LEONARD. Sorry.

YVONNE. But we couldn't let him have a mistress before I have a lover, could we?

LEONARD. No? Couldn't we?

YVONNE. No, we couldn't. So I'll join you tonight.

LEONARD. (*Almost falls off stool.*) Good heavens . . . no! It wouldn't be right. You see, he's my friend.

YVONNE. Does that stop him from spending the night with your wife?

LEONARD. Well, just because he's impolite to me, doesn't mean I should be rude to him!

YVONNE. I'm joining you tonight! That's all there is to it!

LEONARD. How will I sleep? If you think I'm going to waste that pill . . . !

YVONNE. Tonight!

JACQUES. (*He enters from dining room.*) Dinner is served, madame!

YVONNE. (*To* LEONARD.) Shall we return to the others? (LEONARD *nods.*) And behave as though nothing's happened.

LEONARD. What's going to happen to me in the dark?

YVONNE. You'll see, Moumou. You'll see!

LEONARD. But that's just it, I *won't* see, and I'm afraid you'll take advantage!

(JACQUES *steps aside to let* YVONNE *and* LEONARD *exit dining room.* INSPECTOR LEGRAND *enters from hall determined to do his duty.*)

INSPECTOR. (*Gruffly.*) Come here!

JACQUES. (*Turning around frightened.*) Huh? Who are you?

INSPECTOR. Police!

JACQUES. Police?

INSPECTOR. Quiet! I know everything!

JACQUES. (*Uneasily.*) You do?

INSPECTOR. I have all the information I need.
Latouche is mine! Do you have anything to say?

JACQUES. (*Hopelessly.*) Nothing. If you know everything . . . do your duty.

INSPECTOR. (*Menacingly, as he feels in his pocket.*)
That's what I'm going to do.

JACQUES. (*Aside.*) Handcuffs!

INSPECTOR. (*Gruffly.*) Come here! (JACQUES *sub-
missively offers his wrists as he crosses to him.*) Here's
a hundred francs!

JACQUES. Why?

INPECTOR. Because I always line up the servants
first. That's my method.

JACQUES. (*At ease.*) A wonderful method! (*Takes
money.*)

INSPECTOR. Do you know him?

JACQUES. Who?

INSPECTOR. Jacques Latouche.

JACQUES. Yes, a little.

INSPECTOR. Where is he?

JACQUES. With my wife!

INSPECTOR. Your wife?

JACQUES. I mean his wife.

INSPECTOR. Chauvinet introduced her to me.
Flaunted her under my nose. What contempt for the
law!

JACQUES. You know I wouldn't be surprised if
Chauvinet isn't an accomplice of this Latouche.

INSPECTOR. Neither would I! I'm going to get them
both tonight!

JACQUES. Both! Latouche *and* Chauvinet! What a
good idea!

INSPECTOR. I may need you to get the handcuffs on
these swindlers! Come with me!

JACQUES. As you say, Inspector! (*They are about
to exit dining room, when* CLAUDINE *enters from hall.*)

CLAUDINE. Inspector! Where are you going?

INSPECTOR. To arrest Jacques Latouche!

CLAUDINE. You can't! Not yet! Not until I get mixed

up in this scandal! I want my share of the publicity!

INSPECTOR. But suppose he escapes while you're getting mixed up? (*To* JACQUES.) Bring them in!

JACQUES. Yes, Inspector! (*Exits dining room.*)

CLAUDINE. But you can't arrest him now. You promised!

INSPECTOR. Promises, promises!

CLAUDINE. Ooh! And you a policeman!

INSPECTOR. But think of my reputation!

CLAUDINE. Think of *my* career! Please let me have just one night. I have it all worked out.

INSPECTOR. What are you planning to do?

CLAUDINE. That would be telling! (*Putting her arms around him.*) Oh, don't refuse me, Inspector or I'll be crushed! Crushed! Do you hear?

INSPECTOR. Yes. I'm getting a faint signal in my antenna!

(YVONNE *enters from dining room, followed by* GEORGES, LEONARD, BABETTE *and* JACQUES. *They line up in that order.*)

CLAUDINE. Here they are!

YVONNE. You wish to see us, Inspector?

INSPECTOR. Yes! Somebody's got himself in deep water . . . up to his neck!

LEONARD. (*Low to* GEORGES.) He's hinting about the swimming instructor!

YVONNE. I don't understand.

GEORGES. Neither do I.

LEONARD. Well, I certainly don't!

BABETTE. (*With a glance at* JACQUES.) Nor I!

INSPECTOR. We will verify the identity of the persons present! (*Turning to* CLAUDINE.) Let me see your Identity Card.

CLAUDINE. (*Digging into bodice.*) Here it is . . . (INSPECTOR *checks card.* YVONNE *watches him.*)

LEONARD. (*Low to* GEORGES.) Say I'm Latouche!

GEORGES. (*Low to* LEONARD.) Of course I will . . .

JACQUES. (*Low to* BABETTE.) Don't give me away!

BABETTE. (*Low to* JACQUES.) Keep quiet!

INSPECTOR. (*Returning card to* CLAUDINE.) Thank you! (*To* YVONNE.) I know you, madame. (*To* GEORGES.) You too . . . At least I thought I knew you.

GEORGES. Meaning?

INSPECTOR. You'll find out soon enough . . . (*To* LEONARD.) Ah! And you?

LEONARD. Me? . . . I'm an old friend of Monsieur Chauvinet.

GEORGES. My old friend Latouche!

INSPECTOR. I am speaking to *this* gentleman!

LEONARD. That's right. I'm his old friend Latouche from Bayeux . . . Jacques Latouche!

INSPECTOR. Are you sure?

LEONARD. (*Pointing to* BABETTE.) Ask my wife! Am I or am I not your husband, Babette dear?

BABETTE. (*After glancing at* JACQUES, *who nudges her to answer.*) Of course you're my husband!

LEONARD. (*To* JACQUES.) Her husband!

JACQUES. (*Sighing with relief.*) Of course you are!

(*They are in the following order:* JACQUES, BABETTE, LEONARD, INSPECTOR, GEORGES, YVONNE *and* CLAUDINE.)

INSPECTOR. (*To* LEONARD.) Your Identity Card!

LEONARD. (*Feeling in his pockets.*) My card . . .

GEORGES. Yes, your Identity Card!

LEONARD. I don't know where I put it!

JACQUES. (*To* BABETTE, *passing her his card.*) Pass it on!

BABETTE. (*Takes card and passes it to* LEONARD.) Pass it on!

LEONARD. (*Slipping card to* INSPECTOR.) Pass it on!

INSPECTOR. Pass it on! Oh, no! I've got it! (*Verifying card.*) Latouche . . . Jacques. No mistake! I hate mistakes!

LEONARD. Satisfied?

INSPECTOR. Yes! You may consider yourself under arrest!

LEONARD. (*Frightened.*) Me?

GEORGES. Him!

YVONNE. Oh!

INSPECTOR. (*To* GEORGES.) And you're going to pay for hiding him here in your villa! (*To* LEONARD.) Is he your accomplice?

LEONARD. My accomplice? Look here, Inspector, he's as straight as a die! And so am I!

INSPECTOR. What about those checks? (JACQUES *and* BABETTE *exchange glances.*)

LEONARD. What checks?

INSPECTOR. The ones that bounced!

LEONARD. Oh, Georges, you never told me you made rubber checks!

INSPECTOR. (*To* LEONARD.) You can explain everything to the judge!

LEONARD. In that case, I prefer to tell the truth! I am not Jacques Latouche!

INSPECTOR. What?

LEONARD. I am not from Bayeux!

YVONNE. Georges, you lied to me! He is not your old friend. He is not Jacques Latouche! He is not from Bayeux!

LEONARD. Of course I'm not, am I, Georges?

GEORGES. (*Desperately.*) But he is, darling! He is!

LEONARD. (*Indignantly.*) Oh, Georges! Aren't you ashamed? (*Stamps foot.*)

INSPECTOR. (*To* BABETTE.) Then he's not your husband, madame?

BABETTE. But he is, Inspector! Believe me, he is!

JACQUES. Yes! He's been telling me over and over!

LEONARD. (*To* INSPECTOR.) No, I'm not the man you think I am!

INSPECTOR. You're lying! All the witnesses agree! (*Suddenly pointing to* LEONARD's *case on bar.*) Whose case is that? Who does it belong to?

LEONARD. That's mine!

INSPECTOR. (*Triumphantly holding up the case.*) Exactly! You convicted yourself. Look at those initials: L.J. . . . . Latouche, Jacques!

LEONARD. L.J.! Oh, I'm just a plaything of the gods! . . . (*Recovering.*) But my real name is Leonard Jolijoli!

JACQUES. What?

CLAUDINE. Nonsense! (*Pointing to* JACQUES.) That's Leonard Jolijoli . . . the butler!

JACQUES. Here's my Identity Card, Inspector!

LEONARD. (*Making grab for card.*) It's mine!

INSPECTOR. Hands off!

LEONARD. What a brute you are!

INSPECTOR. (*Taking card.*) Give it to me! Leonard Jolijoli. It's in order! (*Returns card to* JACQUES *and turns to* LEONARD.) That finishes you! You're under arrest! Tonight you sleep in jail!

LEONARD. Oh, no!

YVONNE. But not tonight, Inspector! Please!

BABETTE. No, not tonight! Please! (YVONNE *and* BABETTE *continue frantically with* "no, no, no," "please," *etc.*)

INSPECTOR. All right. All right, ladies! For your sakes! But I warn you the villa is under constant surveillance. He can stay here tonight, but tomorrow . . . jail! (INSPECTOR *and* CLAUDINE *exit hall.* YVONNE *and* BABETTE *turn to their quarry,* LEONARD, *and close in on him during the following, until they have him trapped on the couch at the curtain.*)

BABETTE. Moumou . . .

YVONNE. Monsieur Latouche . . . We saved you!

BABETTE. *For tonight!*

YVONNE. Your last night of freedom!

BABETTE. You won't regret a moment of it!

LEONARD. (*Desperately.*) Inspector! *Inspector!*

CURTAIN

ACT THREE

The living room of the Villa Clair de Lune. Next morning. GEORGES *is alone. He appears to be anxiously awaiting someone. A moment later he moves quickly to hall to meet* INSPECTOR LEGRAND, *who enters hurriedly with the same busy and important air.*

INSPECTOR. Good morning!

GEORGES. Oh, Inspector, I've been waiting for you!

INSPECTOR. Hoping I wouldn't show up? Right?

GEORGES. Look, Inspector, I didn't get much sleep last night.

INSPECTOR. No wonder. You've got yourself in quite a situation, Chauvinet!

GEORGES. I don't see what you have against me.

INSPECTOR. I suppose you had no idea what your old friend Latouche was up to?

GEORGES. Not the slightest. Believe me.

INSPECTOR. (*Ironically.*) You didn't even know he existed. Right?

GEORGES. (*Ready to admit all.*) That's it exactly, Inspector. You may not believe this . . . but I don't even know Jacques Latouche.

INSPECTOR. For two months this swindler's been on the wanted list. I find him hiding out here . . . in your house . . . and you say you don't even know him.

GEORGES. It's true, I tell you, I . . . Look, as a special favor to me, hush up this Latouche affair for the next few days.

INSPECTOR. Hush it up?! I'm going to blow it up . . . inflate it . . . turn it into a work of art . . . like a Venetian glass blower!

68

GEORGES. Oh! . . . No!

(INSPECTOR *goes to phone.* GEORGES *is in dire despair.* JACQUES *enters from hall, wearing raincoat and bowler hat.*)

JACQUES. (*To* GEORGES.) Good morning, m'sieur. Sorry if I'm late . . . I had a few things to . . . (GEORGES *gestures him to stop talking so he can listen to the* INSPECTOR.)

INSPECTOR. Quiet! (*Into phone.*) Hello! Get me the Normandie Sun . . . Inspector Legrand speaking. Give me the editor. (*Sings first line of "The Marseillaise."*) "Ye sons of France arise to glory" . . . Ah, Pierre, I have more on that story I gave you last night . . . Yes, for the special noon edition . . . Headline: Scandal in Deauville. Under that: Inspector Legrand puts his foot in a sewer . . . Yes, I said sewer. Sewer of vice!

GEORGES. (*Staggered.*) Now see here, Inspector!

INSPECTOR. Quiet! (*Into phone.*) This sewer is the villa of a distinguished resident, where the notorious swindler, Jacques Latouche, has been hiding out.

JACQUES. (*Aside.*) Whew!

INSPECTOR. (*Into phone.*) This Latouche, not satisfied with swindling the good citizens of Normandie, has seduced and debauched an adorable young girl, the pure and innocent Claudine Amour.

JACQUES. That's a lie!

INSPECTOR. (*Threateningly.*) What?

JACQUES. I said: Oh, my! (*Removes hat; covers heart.*)

INSPECTOR. (*Into phone.*) According to the young victim, secret orgies take place in this infamous villa. The butler sleeps in the husband's bed . . . so the wife, no doubt, can join him there . . .

GEORGES. You're going to ruin me!

JACQUES. Me, too!

INSPECTOR. Quiet! (*Into phone.*) While the husband

takes his pleasures in Madame Latouche's bed! . . .
Yes, with the swindler's wife! (*With a chuckle.*) That
should do it! Get the presses rolling, Pierre! (*Hangs
up.*) They'll be talking about Inspector Legrand before
this day is over! Where's the prisoner?

GEORGES. I haven't seen him yet. He's still sleeping.

JACQUES. In the spare room.

GEORGES. On goose feathers.

INSPECTOR. Well, to each his own. (*Looks at watch.*)
I'll be back in no time . . . with the police wagon!
(*Exits hall, leaving* GEORGES *and* JACQUES *in despair.*)

JACQUES. Well, that finishes it.

GEORGES. *You* have nothing to worry about.

JACQUES. I was thinking of poor old Jacques! What
terrible publicity!

GEORGES. The hell with poor old Jacques! If I ever
get my hands on him . . . ! (*Puts hands around*
JACQUES' *neck.*) Oh! Excuse me! (*Furiously.*) And
that maid!

JACQUES. She must have seen me going into your
bedroom last night.

GEORGES. But I was only out of it for a short spell.

JACQUES. (*Anxiously.*) Yes, but . . . er . . . during that time, did you meet with any success with
Madame Latouche?

GEORGES. No! She refused to open the door, shouting: "What's the matter with little sister? Isn't *her*
motor going?" (JACQUES *laughs contentedly.*) Do you
know what she meant?

JACQUES. No.

GEORGES. Neither do I. Then why are you laughing?

JACQUES. (*Sadly.*) Because I feel sorry for you,
m'sieur.

GEORGES. Hmm. Just who are you?

JACQUES. Me? . . . Leonard Jolijoli.

GEORGES. Hah!

JACQUES. Unless monsieur can prove otherwise!

GEORGES. Hmm. (LEONARD *enters from hall, wearing
a flowered dressing gown over his pajamas.*) Ah, here

comes our drooping lily now! (LEONARD *is anything but drooping. He bounces in, going to the French windows where he does knee bends, then jumps over the sofa.*)

LEONARD. Morning, Georges! Morning, butler!

JACQUES. (*Bowing.*) M'sieur . . . (*To* GEORGES.) I shall return to my duties, m'sieur.

GEORGES. Yes, go!

LEONARD. Yes, go, Leonard! For I suppose you're still Leonard Jolijoli!

JACQUES. If you don't have any objections, Monsieur Jacques Latouche!

LEONARD. None, my man. None. (JACQUES *exits dining room.*)

GEORGES. If it wasn't for my wife, I wouldn't have to put up with any of this . . .

LEONARD. What?

GEORGES. It's her money in my business. If she divorces me, I'll be in a hell of a mess!

LEONARD. You're already in a hell of a mess!

GEORGES. Listen, Leonard, for both our sakes you must disappear!

LEONARD. Me?

GEORGES. (*Taking out money from wallet.*) Here's a thousand francs. You can slip out by the side door, while the Inspector's man covers the front of the house. He won't see you. It's easy.

LEONARD. I'm to run away?

GEORGES. It's the only solution. If you slip through his fingers, the Inspector won't dare do anything more about this affair. We'll both be saved. Quick! Go and get dressed! Here's the money!

LEONARD. (*Taking money.*) If you insist! But there's no question of my leaving!

GEORGES. Think of the scandal . . . the Comedie Francaise!

LEONARD. Comedie Francaise . . . Scandal . . . Pooh! From now on, I'm interested in only one thing!

GEORGES. What's that?

LEONARD. (*Twirling tassel of dressing gown.*) *Women!*

GEORGES. What did you say?

LEONARD. Or to be more precise . . . *the* woman! The one and only enchantress who last night revealed to me all the ways of love!

GEORGES. (*Amazed.*) All the ways of love!

LEONARD. (*In chair Left Center, he slides down until his back and head reach the floor, his feet in air.*) Yes! I was lying in my room . . . your wonderful lightless room. I was just beginning to dream . . . when suddenly I realized it wasn't a dream at all. She was there and I succumbed . . . succumbed deliciously into nameless bliss!

GEORGES. Who was she?

LEONARD. (*Still upside down in the chair.*) I don't know!

GEORGES. You don't know?

LEONARD. Shrouded in darkness, in the silent watches of the night, she was silent, too! As for me, my lips were sealed with bliss too thrilling for words! . . . When I awoke, she had vanished!

GEORGES. Who was this miracle worker?

LEONARD. Your wife . . .

GEORGES. My wife?

LEONARD. Or Babette.

GEORGES. Babette! You have the nerve to tell me you're the lover of my wife or my future mistress!

LEONARD. Why not! They both warned me they were going to spend the night with me!

GEORGES. No. You're making this up!

LEONARD. (*Rises.*) You tried to deceive Yvonne and you lied to Babette when you said you weren't married. Naturally, they wanted to get back at you. And just between us, Georges, I think you deserved it!

GEORGES. No. Babette wouldn't do this to me!

LEONARD. If it's Babette, I'm keeping her for myself!

GEORGES. Oh, are you? And if it's my wife?

LEONARD. You will bifurcate!

GEORGES. I will what?

LEONARD. You will bifurcate!

GEORGES. By myself?

LEONARD. Yes, and leave her with me!

GEORGES. That's ridiculous!

LEONARD. I warn you, I'm a man who takes what's coming to him! By force, if necessary!

GEORGES. Now, now, Leonard. Make an effort! Try to remember which one it was!

LEONARD. I'm doing my best! After all, I'm the one it concerns most!

GEORGES. You!

LEONARD. Yes, and when I know which one it is, I'll give you ample warning which one *not* to expect back! Now if you'll excuse me, I'll go an get dressed! (*Crosses to hall.*)

GEORGES. Look here, Leonard, please try to remember! I beg of you in the name of our friendship . . . (*Picks up flower.*) the sacred cult of friendship! Isn't friendship sweeter than love? (*Gives flower to* LEONARD, *as* LEONARD *gave it to him in the first act.*)

LEONARD. Friendship! Oh, you poor little Bo Peep! There's only one thing that counts . . . love! Ah, if you only knew what love is! (*Puts flower between teeth.*) Arrumph! (*Kicks foot behind him and exits hall.*)

GEORGES. I do! And I didn't have to wait until last night to find out! . . . Oh, that two-timing bachelor! (LEONARD *pops his head back into room.*)

LEONARD. I have a clue, Georges!

GEORGES. You have?

LEONARD. She was wearing those pajama things . . . no bottoms . . . all tops.

GEORGES. Any woman who would go around wearing only pajama tops would . . .

LEONARD. (*Knowingly.*) Yes, she would, Georges.

GEORGES. But I don't know anyone who wears pajama tops.

LEONARD. Find out, old boy! Find out! (*Head pops out of sight.*)

YVONNE. (*She enters from study.*) Ah! There you are! You're never in your room, are you?

GEORGES. Yvonne, I have a question to ask you!

YVONNE. After me! . . . What was the butler doing in your bed last night?

GEORGES. (*Innocently.*) He was in my bed?

YVONNE. That wasn't your beard I saw on the pillow!

GEORGES. The butler? No! It's not possible!

YVONNE. Don't lie. You used that dummy so you could spend the night with that Madame Latouche creature!

GEORGES. I swear to you, darling, I haven't deceived you!

YVONNE. But you wanted to! And when I found out, I was so hurt . . . I needed someone to comfort me. And suddenly I remembered the words: "An eye for an eye . . . a Latouche for a Latouche!" So I went to Monsieur Latouche.

GEORGES. Yvonne, you didn't! He has just confessed to me that last night someone stole into his room, but in the darkness he couldn't identify her . . . except for the pajamas she was wearing.

YVONNE. Pajamas? How cute!

GEORGES. But you don't wear pajamas . . . do you? You never have . . . have you?

YVONNE. Well . . . nót the old kind, Georges.

GEORGES. Thank God!

YVONNE. Just these . . . the tops. (*Opens negligee, revealing pajama tops.*)

GEORGES. (*In agony.*) No-o-o! But it wasn't you! Say it wasn't you!

YVONNE. (*Defiantly.*) It *was* me!

GEORGES. I don't believe it!

YVONNE. Then I shall go back to him . . . right now . . . and pick up where we left off!

GEORGES. No! I forbid it! I demand a complete explanation!

YVONNE. With pleasure. I'll give you all the intimate details!

CLAUDINE. (*She enters from hall.*) Here's the morning paper! If madame would care to read what it says about the villa . . .

YVONNE. Thank you, I've already read it. (*To* GEORGES.) And I warn you, Georges, if any scandal breaks out, I'll pack my bags, take my money and get a divorce! (*Exits hall.*)

GEORGES. Scandal! How can it be avoided?

CLAUDINE. (*Offering him unfolded newspaper.*) Would you like to see it, m'sieur?

GEORGES. (*Anxiously.*) Is my name mentioned?

CLAUDINE. Not yet. The names of the accomplices won't come out until the noon edition.

GEORGES. (*Looking at watch.*) My God! It's almost noon now!

CLAUDINE. (*Showing him newspaper article.*) See . . . three large question marks. That's Jacques Latouche on one side, Leonard Jolijoli on the other . . . and me . . . the luscious Claudine Amour . . . bang in the middle!

GEORGES. So all this is for you . . . and I'm the scapegoat!

CLAUDINE. It would have been wiser, m'sieur, if you had set me up in a pretty little apartment with five thousand francs the first of every month . . . (*Provocatively.*) Not to mention certain pleasures you could have received in return . . . for, if I may say so, I have now perfected myself in every phase of my profession.

GEORGES. (*Putting his arm around her and patting*

her appropriately.) Ah, yes . . . you have blossomed, my dear. I should have noticed earlier. But it's never too late . . .

CLAUDINE. It isn't?

GEORGES. Not for the apartment, it isn't. That could be arranged. But you have to tell Inspector Legrand you made a terrible mistake.

CLAUDINE. (*Innocently*.) But monsieur . . . that would be dishonest.

GEORGES. (*Holding her tighter*.) Ten thousand francs a month?

CLAUDINE. I'll be dishonest!

BABETTE. (*She enters from hall*.) I hope I'm not disturbing you?

CLAUDINE. Not at all! I was just discussing with monsieur . . .

GEORGES. Yes! I was telling Claudine how to be brave in face of this awful scandal . . .

CLAUDINE. Yes, madame, it pays to be brave.

BABETTE. And can you be a brave little girl and bring my breakfast? And my husband's?

CLAUDINE. The butler will bring it, madame. (*Exits dining room*.)

GEORGES. Babette! Thank God, at last I can talk to you! What did you mean by my little sister and her motor?

BABETTE. Your little sister! She breaks my heart!

GEORGES. Why didn't you let me in last night?

BABETTE. Because your wife confided in me and now I know all about your amorous carburetors!

GEORGES. Our carburetors? You only wanted to get back at me! Leonard told me all about it. You suggested he spend the night with you!

BABETTE. And suppose I did?

GEORGES. An unknown female slipped into his room in the dark . . .

BABETTE. How interesting! . . . And he doesn't know who it was?

GEORGES. Tell me . . . what do you have under that negligee?

BABETTE. Really, Georges! That's something you'll never discover!

GEORGES. Do you wear pajamas?

BABETTE. Do I look the type who'd wear . . . (*Stops short, gives him a teasing smile and crosses legs, allowing a bare one to be seen.*)

GEORGES. Well, you don't wear the bottoms.

BABETTE. No, I don't, Georges. (JACQUES *enters with breakfast for two. He sees* GEORGES *staring at* BABETTE's *leg. Rises.*) But I do wear the tops! (*Opens negligee and models pajama tops.*) Cool, comfortable and congenial!

JACQUES. (*Angrily slams tray on table.*) *Oh!*

BABETTE. Service with a smile.

GEORGES. Will someone tell me what's going on around here?

BABETTE. Ask the butler. Perhaps he knows.

GEORGES. How would he know?

JACQUES. Quite so, m'sieur. Madame has asked for her bags. She says she's going home to mother!

GEORGES. But she can't! She mustn't!

BABETTE. That's right, run after her! Don't stay because of me!

GEORGES. (*Distraught.*) But she's my wife! *You* understand!

BABETTE. Oh, get out of here!

GEORGES. Take it from me, butler, never get married! (*Exits quickly hall.*)

JACQUES. Now he tells me! . . . If you're going to model for anyone, it will be for me!

BABETTE. Not exclusively.

JACQUES. Be careful, Babette! . . . I've got great news! I went to the Casino last night . . .

BABETTE. Still gambling?

JACQUES. . . . with five hundred francs the maid advanced me!

BABETTE. So now you're swindling the maid!

JACQUES. Yes, but I won back twice as much as I lost!

BABETTE. Then you can make good your checks?

JACQUES. I've already called up the manager of the bank. He's contacting my creditors . . .

BABETTE. Will they withdraw their complaints against you?

JACQUES. I don't know yet. He's going to call me back. Until then no one must know who I am.

BABETTE. Of course not! But if you've been lucky at the tables, it's thanks to me. You know what they say: "Unlucky in love . . ."

JACQUES. What do you mean?

BABETTE. I've been unfaithful to you, Jacques! Unfaithful!

JACQUES. It's not true, Babette! Monsieur Chauvinet remained outside in the corridor! You wouldn't open your door!

BABETTE. (*Furiously.*) Oh! So he told you! But he's not the only man in this house! Look around!

JACQUES. Where? (LEONARD, *fully dressed, enters from hall.*)

BABETTE. There!

JACQUES. Him!

LEONARD. Good morning, darling! You're as dewy fresh as a rose this morning!

BABETTE. Did you sleep well? (LEONARD *kisses her hand.*)

LEONARD. (*Rapturously.*) Very badly, thank you! . . . God, I'm hungry!

BABETTE. So am I. All right, butler. You may serve us! Sit here close to me, darling. (JACQUES *suffers.*)

LEONARD. It's exquisite being the darling of an adorable woman!

BABETTE. How tender you are this morning, my love!

LEONARD. I was so happy last night . . .

BABETTE. I know . . .

LEONARD. What? You know?

BABETTE. Of course. Am I not your wife, my treasure?

LEONARD. Of course you are. But last night we went beddie bye bye in separate rooms.

BABETTE. Yes, I know we went beddie bye bye in separate rooms . . . but I got up . . . and surprised you in the dark.

LEONARD. (*Ecstatically.*) You? . . . It was you?

BABETTE. Yes, it was me, Moumou.

LEONARD. Oh, how happy you've made me! Then I haven't been unfaithful to you, my darling wife?

BABETTE. Of course not, my dearest husband!

LEONARD. We kept it in the family!! . . . What could be nicer than that!

JACQUES. Am I in the way?

BABETTE. Not at all!

LEONARD. I want *everyone* to know how happy I am! (*Carried away.*) And I owe it all to her! To Babette! Do you hear?

JACQUES. I hear!

LEONARD. Pack your things, my darling! I've plenty of money now! We'll run away together!

JACQUES. What? You're going away with her?

LEONARD. Is she or is she not my wife?

JACQUES. Yes, m'sieur.

LEONARD. And heaven help the man who dares come between us! I'd kill him like a dog! Understand?

JACQUES. Oh! Yes, m'sieur.

LEONARD. Hurry, darling! Let's get out of here before that fool of an Inspector shows up!

BABETTE. Yes. Why not? Why shouldn't I?

LEONARD. I can't wait to be alone with you again! I'm so far behind! . . . It's so beautiful! So good! I adore you!

BABETTE. All right. I'm coming with you. Ten minutes and I'm yours! (*Exits hall, throwing him a kiss.*)

LEONARD. (*To* JACQUES.) Stop standing there like a worn out tooth brush! (*Slight pause; then, aggres-*

sively.) *Pack my bag* and be *quick* about it! (JACQUES *exits.* LEONARD, *strutting like the conquering hero.*) Love is rough and violent! Nothing like it to give you an appetite! (*Pours and holds up cup of coffee.*) "Coffee after such a night is the warrior's delight!" (*Drinks.*)

YVONNE. (*She enters from hall.*) Oh! Is it you, dear Monsieur Latouche?

LEONARD. (*Ecstatically.*) Ah, madame! What a beautiful thing is life! Behold in me the favored of the gods!

YVONNE. I'm so happy for you!

LEONARD. What an unforgettable night I have spent under your roof!

YVONNE. I'm very glad.

LEONARD. I venture no details, for you cannot imagine . . .

YVONNE. Must I imagine? My memory isn't that short . . .

LEONARD. (*Surprised.*) What's that?

YVONNE. We're alone . . . besides my husband knows everything!

LEONARD. Everything?

YVONNE. You told him you had a visitor last night . . .

LEONARD. Yes . . . and I know who it was!

YVONNE. Thank you for not telling him . . . but I *had* to tell him the truth!

LEONARD. What truth?

YVONNE. Georges wanted to become your wife's lover.

LEONARD. Oh, that.

YVONNE. So it was only right for you to do the same to him!

LEONARD. What!

YVONNE. And since I did what I did to get my revenge, I had to let him know I was your mistress!

LEONARD. You? It was you?

YVONNE. Now he knows what it feels like to be deceived . . . and I can't say that I'm sorry . . . after the way he was trying to make a fool of me.

LEONARD. Well, I'll be damned!

YVONNE. What?

LEONARD. I know there was one . . . and that was extraordinary enough. But now you say there were two!

YVONNE. Two what?

LEONARD. Is it possible that I fell asleep . . . and was the happy victim of a double surprise?

YVONNE. Tell me one thing, do you have the courage of your convictions?

LEONARD. I thought I'd given you proof of that last night.

YVONNE. Then tell my husband you're my lover. He seems to think you're incapable of it!

LEONARD. So he doubts my ability, does he? The damn fool! I'll show him! Are you sure it was you?

YVONNE. Didn't I tell you I would be there?

LEONARD. Yes, that's right, you did.

YVONNE. Well?

LEONARD. I feel as excited as a young hunter who's bagged two birds on his first time out! What are we going to do?

YVONNE. Oh, I'm leaving!

LEONARD. Not without me!

YVONNE. But I'm going home to mama!

LEONARD. That's fine. We'll go together. My capacity for love is unlimited!

YVONNE. But mama is old-fashioned.

LEONARD. I'll soon fix that!

YVONNE. All the same . . .

LEONARD. (*Embracing her.*) Now that I've found you, I'm not going to lose you! It's too beautiful! Too good! I adore you!

GEORGES. (*He enters.*) Hm! Are you two still playing at being lovers?

YVONNE. We are lovers! I spent the night with him!

GEORGES. You couldn't have done such an infamous thing!

LEONARD. Georges, if you only knew how lovely it was! You're my friend . . . I wish you could have been there to see how happy I was!

GEORGES. This is going too far!

LEONARD. I told you, Georges . . . I won't give her up . . . (*Advancing on him.*) I'd rather kill you both!

GEORGES. You're crazy!

YVONNE. You're both being very sweet but don't you think I should be consulted?

LEONARD. Certainly not! You're coming with me!

YVONNE. And your wife?

LEONARD. Oh, I'm taking her too!

GEORGES. How about leaving one behind for me?

LEONARD. Sorry, old boy. This morning I didn't know which one it was . . . but it now appears it was both of them!

YVONNE. Both? No!

LEONARD. Yes!

GEORGES. What are you going to do?

LEONARD. What can I do but begin again, compare . . and then choose!

YVONNE. (*Indignantly.*) Oh! . . .

GEORGES. Oh! . . .

(BABETTE *enters from hall, followed by* JACQUES, *carrying bags and looking very disgruntled.*)

BABETTE. (*To* LEONARD.) Darling, I'm all yours! (*Pointing to* JACQUES.) The butler is bringing our bags.

LEONARD. (*To* JACQUES.) Thank you, Leonard. Well, let's be off, my darlings!

BABETTE. Darlings?

LEONARD. Yes, there's three of us. We're going with Madame Chauvinet to her mother's!

BABETTE. Whatever for?

LEONARD. To throw some light on what happened to me in the dark.

YVONNE. (*To* LEONARD.) But Jacques, you know what happened!

BABETTE. (*To* LEONARD.) Yes, I told you exactly! Come on! I've had enough of this villa!

YVONNE. So have I! The three of us can straighten it out together!

LEONARD. Why not?

GEORGES. (*Pleading.*) Yvonne . . . you can't do this to me!

YVONNE. No-o-o?

LEONARD. Come along! Goodbye, Georges!

BABETTE. (*To* JACQUES.) Goodbye, Leonard!

GEORGES. Yvonne! Yvonne!

INSPECTOR. (*He enters.*) Wait a minute! Where do you think you're going?

LEONARD. To find a car.

INSPECTOR. Well, you're in luck! I have one waiting outside . . . with a seat reserved for each one of you!

LEONARD. Oh, no, Inspector . . . not now!

INSPECTOR. The law claims you!

LEONARD. No! Love claims me! (*Pulls* YVONNE *and* BABETTE *close to him.*)

CLAUDINE. (*She enters from hall, wearing a raincoat.*) Hold it, Inspector! Hold it!

INSPECTOR. I've been holding it long enough!

CLAUDINE. But I've just come from the Normandie Sun! My poet is famous!

YVONNE. What poet?

CLAUDINE. Haven't you seen his poems in the paper . . . ? Look! Each one is a masterpiece! (*Crosses to* LEONARD *to* YVONNE *to* BABETTE *with newspapers.*)

LEONARD. My poems!

CLAUDINE. Deauville is buzzing with excitement!

Everyone is asking: who is this mysterious, unknown genius . . . ?

LEONARD. (*Shouting to* GEORGES.) Leonard Jolijoli!

CLAUDINE. (*Pointing to* JACQUES.) And there he is!

YVONNE. The butler?

BABETTE. (*Ironically to* JACQUES.) You're a genius?

JACQUES. How about that!

CLAUDINE. (*Enthusiastically.*) Winner of the First Prize: Leonard Jolijoli!

LEONARD. (*Exultantly.*) Georges, do you hear? It's Leonard Jolijoli!

INSPECTOR. What are you so happy about? You're on your way to jail!

LEONARD. Arrest me and you're going to look ridiculous, Inspector! (*Telephone rings.*)

INSPECTOR. We'll see about that! Come on! Follow me!

CLAUDINE. (*Into phone.*) Hello? . . . Jacques Latouche? (*Passes receiver to* LEONARD.) It's for you . . .

LEONARD. Excuse me, Inspector. Wait in the car! (INSPECTOR *starts to leave and returns. Into phone; impatiently.*) What? . . . The manager of what bank? . . . Complaints? . . . What complaints? . . . You have the wrong party!

JACQUES. (*Stopping* LEONARD *from hanging up.*) It won't hurt you to listen to the man!

LEONARD. (*Into phone.*) The complaints against me have been withdrawn? . . . That's fine but I don't give a damn! . . . No, I'm only interested in two things, women and poetry! . . . Yes, in going from bed to verse! (*Hangs up then quickly picks up the receiver again.*) Sorry about that. (*Hangs up.*)

JACQUES. (*Shouting with joy.*) The complaints have been withdrawn!

INSPECTOR. What complaints?

JACQUES. (*Slapping* LEONARD *on back.*) Jacques Latouche has been cleared!

BABETTE. Is it true?

JACQUES. Yes!

LEONARD. (*Slapping* JACQUES *on back.*) And Leonard Jolijoli is the man of the hour!

JACQUES. (*Overwhelmed with joy.*) Good old Jacques!

LEONARD. And good old Leonard! (*They embrace.* LEONARD *spits out whisker from* JACQUES' *beard.*)

CLAUDINE. Now you're no longer needed here, Inspector!

INSPECTOR. Good Lord . . . the noon edition! This is terrible!

GEORGES. You're going to lose your reputation, Inspector!

INSPECTOR. (*Rushing to hall.*) My God! Maybe there's still time! Stop the presses! (*Exits.*)

LEONARD. (*To* JACQUES.) Now you can give me back my Identity Card!

JACQUES. What? Then you're Leonard?

LEONARD. Yes, me!

JACQUES. And you can hand over my Identity Card!

LEONARD. What? You? . . . Jacques!

JACQUES. That's me!

GEORGES. Jacques Latouche? (*To* BABETTE.) Him? The butler?

BABETTE. Yes, that's him, your old friend, Jacques Latouche from Bayeux!

YVONNE. What does this mean?

GEORGES. I wish I knew!

YVONNE. Well, it's clear to me, Georges. You've made a fool of me! I'm leaving you!

BABETTE. (*To* JACQUES.) And I'm leaving you!

JACQUES. No, you're not! I'm leaving you!

GEORGES. And I'm leaving you, Yvonne. After all, in my house with my best friend!

YVONNE. And I'm proud of it!

BABETTE. Nonsense! It was I . . . yes, I . . . who spent the night with him!

CLAUDINE. But you're both mistaken. This man is *my* lover!

LEONARD. What do you mean . . . your lover?

GEORGES. (*To* CLAUDINE.) Do you wear pajamas?

CLAUDINE. The tops. Only the tops. (*Opens her raincoat and models pajama tops.*)

GEORGES. (*To* LEONARD.) Well, you can put another notch on your gun!

LEONARD. But I must know the truth!

GEORGES. Yes . . . the truth!

YVONNE. (*To* GEORGES.) If I have done what I have done, you deserved it!

BABETTE. (*To* JACQUES.) You asked for it . . . (*To* GEORGES.) And so did you!

LEONARD. Two is all right . . . but three!!! . . . What's the record, Georges?

GEORGES. We'll never know which one it was!

JACQUES. Never!

LEONARD. Happiness brushed me with her wings . . . and I was unable to grasp her. Ah, cruel fate! . . . Do you remember how I put it last night?

BABETTE, YVONNE, and CLAUDINE. Oh, yes!

LEONARD.

"Like two halves of an almond, tight in their shell,
  Let us sleep, closely pressed, in our own sweet hell . . .

CLAUDINE. (*Continuing.*)

"For you'll up and leave me tomorrow at seven,
  My body on earth but my soul up in heaven!"

LEONARD. My verse! Only she who shared my couch could know it! (*Taking her in his arms.*) Claudine! It was you!

CLAUDINE. Of course it was me!

GEORGES. Yvonne, you lied to me! You haven't deceived me!

YVONNE. Of course not, darling!

JACQUES. Babette, you didn't deceive me!

BABETTE. (*With a wicked laugh.*) How could I, Jacques?

CLAUDINE. Moumou . . .

LEONARD. There is no more Moumou! I'm Bullbull now! (*Kisses her.*)

CURTAIN

PROPERTY PLOT

cigar
pocket cigarette lighter
table cigarette lighter
3 envelopes containing letters
magazine
beach bag
small overnight bag
small case with the *large* initials "L. J." on it
beach towel
liquor bottle
2 glasses for whiskey
vase with roses
telephone
telegram
cigarette case with cigarettes
cigarette box with cigarettes
wine decanter
4 glasses for sherry wine
3 large suitcases
3 hat boxes
golf clubs
tennis racket
pair of skiis
4 decorative pillows
book
small hand bell for summoning butler
2 wallets
2 identity cards
several sheets of paper with poetry
paper French francs
pill box
water carafe and glass
3 French newspapers
breakfast tray
2 cups and saucers
silver coffee pot
2 teaspoons

NEWSPAPER QUOTES

The Longest, Laugh-Running French Comedy Hit!
3 Years in Paris, 5 Years in Hollywood, 10 Years
from Coast-to-Coast . . . And 6 Years in London!

Pajama Tops—"The most hilarious adult comedy in years"—
Los Angeles News

Pajama Tops—"Should run forever and probably will"—*Los
Angeles Examiner*

Pajama Tops—"In the Hellzapoppin' tradition . . . a zany
evening in the theatre"—*Los Angeles Mirror*

Pajama Tops—"Perfectly wonderful"—McClain, *N.Y. Journal
American*

Pajama Tops—"Prolonged laughter"—*N.Y. Times*

Pajama Tops—"First Nighters Howled"—Coleman, *N.Y.
Mirror*

Pajama Tops—"It's a pure theatrical experience . . . the best
entertainment in London"—John Osborne, *London Sunday
Times*

Pajama Tops—"Utterly mad spoof of the French bedroom
farce"— Mockridge, *N.Y. World-Telegram & Sun*

Pajama Tops—"Has been titillating the nation for more than
a decade. A delight"—Lewis, *Cue*

Pajama Tops—"A pristine specimen of French bedroom farce.
It has a quaint charm, innocence and is laugh provoking"
—*Newsweek*

Pajama Tops—"That classic French farce—fine and funny—
is with us again"—Whittaker, *Toronto Globe*

Pajama Tops—"A hardy perennial with a colorful blossom"—
Robe, *Daily Variety*

Pajama Tops—"A theatrical phenomenon—an absolute comedy
must"—*Seattle Times*

Pajama Tops—"Just what the laugh doctor ordered"—*Miami
Herald*

Pajama Tops—"Comedy highlight of the year"—Variety
correspondent, *Johannesburg, South Africa*

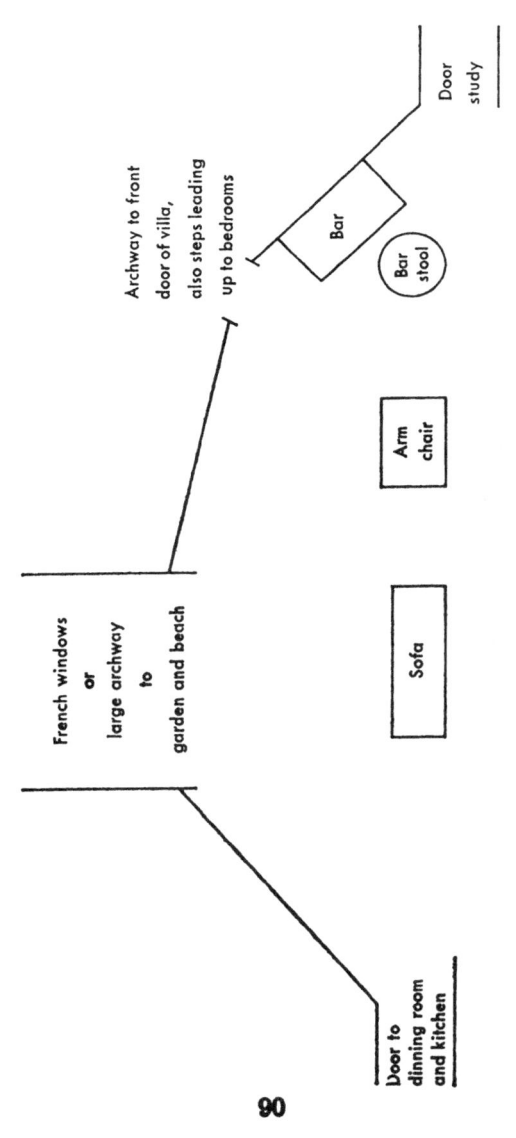

Archway to front
door of villa,
also steps leading
up to bedrooms

Bar

Bar
stool

Door
study

Arm
chair

Sofa

French windows
or
large archway
to
garden and beach

Door to
dinning room
and kitchen

90

Also By

Mawby Green and Ed Feilbert

13 RUE DE L'AMOUR

DING DONG

IN ONE BED... AND OUT THE OTHER

OTHER TITLES AVAILABLE FROM SAMUEL FRENCH

NO SEX PLEASE, WE'RE BRITISH
Anthony Marriott and Alistair Foot

Farce / 7 m, 3 f / Interior

A young bride who lives above a bank with her husband who is the assistant manager, innocently sends a mail order off for some Scandinavian glassware. What comes is Scandinavian pornography. The plot revolves around what is to be done with the veritable floods of pornography, photographs, books, films and eventually girls that threaten to engulf this happy couple. The matter is considerably complicated by the man's mother, his boss, a visiting bank inspector, a police superintendent and a muddled friend who does everything wrong in his reluctant efforts to set everything right, all of which works up to a hilarious ending of closed or slamming doors. This farce ran in London over eight years and also delighted Broadway audiences.

"Titillating and topical."
– NBC TV

"A really funny Broadway show."
– ABC TV

SAMUELFRENCH.COM

OTHER TITLES AVAILABLE FROM SAMUEL FRENCH

THE DECORATOR
Donald Churchill

Comedy / 1m, 2f / Interior

Marcia returns to her flat to find it has not been painted as she arranged. A part time painter who is filling in for an ill colleague is just beginning the work when the wife of the man with whom Marcia is having an affair arrives to tell all to Marcia's husband. Marcia hires the painter a part time actor to impersonate her husband at the confrontation. Hilarity is piled upon hilarity as the painter, who takes his acting very seriously, portrays the absent husband. The wronged wife decides that the best revenge is to sleep with Marcia's husband, an ecstatic experience for them both. When Marcia learns that the painter/actor has slept with her rival, she demands the opportunity to show him what really good sex is.

"Irresistible."
– *London Daily Telegraph*

"This play will leave you rolling in the aisles....
I all but fell from my seat laughing."
– *London Star*

SAMUELFRENCH.COM

OTHER TITLES AVAILABLE FROM SAMUEL FRENCH

CAPTIVE
Jan Buttram

Comedy / 2m, 1f / Interior

A hilarious take on a father/daughter relationship, this off beat comedy combines foreign intrigue with down home philosophy. Sally Pound flees a bad marriage in New York and arrives at her parent's home in Texas hoping to borrow money from her brother to pay a debt to gangsters incurred by her husband. Her elderly parents are supposed to be vacationing in Israel, but she is greeted with a shotgun aimed by her irascible father who has been left home because of a minor car accident and is not at all happy to see her. When a news report indicates that Sally's mother may have been taken captive in the Middle East, Sally's hard-nosed brother insists that she keep father home until they receive definite word, and only then will he loan Sally the money. Sally fails to keep father in the dark, and he plans a rescue while she finds she is increasingly unable to skirt the painful truths of her life. The ornery father and his loveable but slightly-dysfunctional daughter come to a meeting of hearts and minds and solve both their problems.

OTHER TITLES AVAILABLE FROM SAMUEL FRENCH

MURDER AMONG FRIENDS
Bob Barry

Comedy thriller / 4m, 2f / Interior

Take an aging, exceedingly vain actor; his very rich wife; a double dealing, double loving agent, plunk them down in an elegant New York duplex and add dialogue crackling with wit and laughs, and you have the basic elements for an evening of pure, sophisticated entertainment. Angela, the wife and Ted, the agent, are lovers and plan to murder Palmer, the actor, during a contrived robbery on New Year's Eve. But actor and agent are also lovers and have an identical plan to do in the wife. A murder occurs, but not one of the planned ones.

"Clever, amusing, and very surprising."
– *New York Times*

"A slick, sophisticated show that is modern and very funny."
– WABC TV

www.ingramcontent.com/pod-product-compliance
Lightning Source LLC
Chambersburg PA
CBHW070635120726
47909CB00004B/1451

* 9 7 8 0 5 7 3 6 1 4 3 9 2 *